Dear Reader,

We have exciting news! As I'm sure you've noticed, the Harlequin Blaze books you know and love have a brand-new look, starting this month. And it's *hot!* Don't you agree?

But don't worry—nothing else about the Blaze books has changed. You'll still find those unforgettable love stories with intrepid heroines, hot, hunky heroes and a double dose of sizzle!

Check out this month's red-hot reads....

#729 THE RISK-TAKER by Kira Sinclair
(Uniformly Hot!)

#730 LYING IN BED by Jo Leigh
(The Wrong Bed)

#731 HIS KIND OF TROUBLE by Samantha Hunter
(The Berringers)

#732 ONE MORE KISS by Kathy Garbera

#733 RELENTLESS SEDUCTION by Jillian Burns

#734 THE WEDDING FLING by Meg Maguire

I hope you're as pleased with our new look as we are. Drop by www.Harlequin.com or www.blazeauthors.com to let us know what you think.

Brenda Chin
Senior Editor
Harlequin Blaze

The Risk-Taker

—

Kira Sinclair

HARLEQUIN®
entertain, enrich, inspire™

Recycling programs
for this product may
not exist in your area.

ISBN-13: 978-0-373-79733-2

THE RISK-TAKER

ABOUT THE AUTHOR

Kira Sinclair's first foray into writing romance was for a high school English assignment. Nothing could dampen her enthusiasm...not even being forced to read about the Scottish laird and his headstrong lass aloud to the class. Although it definitely made her blush. Writing about striking, sexy heroes and passionate, determined women has always excited her. She sold her first book to Harlequin Blaze in 2007 and hasn't looked back. With seven books currently available, and more on the way, she still can't believe she gets to make her living doing something so fun. She loves to hear from readers at www.KiraSinclair.com.

Books by Kira Sinclair

HARLEQUIN BLAZE

415—WHISPERS IN THE DARK
469—AFTERBURN
588—CAUGHT OFF GUARD
605—WHAT MIGHT HAVE BEEN
667—BRING IT ON*
672—TAKE IT DOWN*
680—RUB IT IN*

*Island Nights

To get the inside scoop on Harlequin Blaze and its talented writers, be sure to check out blazeauthors.com.

Other titles by this author available in ebook format.
Don't miss any of our special offers. Write to us at the following address for information on our newest releases.

Harlequin Reader Service
U.S.: 3010 Walden Ave., P.O. Box 1325, Buffalo, NY 14269
Canadian: P.O. Box 609, Fort Erie, Ont. L2A 5X3

I'd like to dedicate this book
to all the men and women who have been wounded
serving and protecting our country. Thank you
for your service. Your sacrifice is not in vain.

1

A HEAVY FIST CONNECTED with his jaw. Gage Harper's head snapped backward and the crowd, pressed tight against the raised platform, roared.

All Gage heard was the rush of adrenaline as it poured through his body. It drowned out the words that had been haunting him all night. "In a war that brings mostly sad news, tonight there is a brighter story to tell." Someone should tell the solemn man who delivered that statement to the world that *bright* and *war* should never be used in the same sentence.

But Gage wasn't going to be the one to do it.

Instead, he squared his feet beneath him and countered the blow he'd received with several of his own. Head, gut, kidneys. This wasn't the sort of place that worried about rules. The backwoods fighting ring was exactly what he needed to distract him from the memories he didn't want.

Micah's flag-draped casket being loaded into the transport for home. A hard-eyed insurgent yelling into his face before ripping both of his thumbnails out

*with pliers. The screams of his friends as they endured
torture.*

Torture he could have prevented if he hadn't screwed
up.

Yeah, this was a great use of a Thursday night even
if he'd had to drive an hour out of Sweetheart, South
Carolina, to find it. The blessed numbness would be
worth every fist to the face.

Grounding his weight onto his left leg, Gage lashed
out with a roundhouse kick. Channeling all the frustration, rage and guilt built up inside him, he put more
power behind it than he'd meant to, aiming straight for
the guy's gut. He was finding it difficult to hold back
after months of fighting for his life. Those kind of hard-
won instincts were a bitch to get rid of. Luckily the
other guy blocked.

Scenes he thought he'd dealt with flashed across his
mind. *Gunfire. Smoke-filled hallways. A dark, dirty
cell with barely enough room to lie down. Tanner, a
fellow Ranger, bloody and broken before they'd even
been thrown into that room, moaning in pain. Needles.
Knives. Pliers.*

But he didn't break. He hadn't told them a damn
thing.

Gage ground his teeth and pushed the memories
away. Nothing could change what had happened to
Tanner.

Or bring Micah back. The man he'd met in jump
school was gone. Killed when his gun misfired while
cleaning it. That, more than anything, was what bothered him about his friend's death. He knew Micah. Had
trained with the man. Micah could disassemble, clean
and reassemble his weapon in his sleep. They all could.

Dying in battle, that he could have dealt with. They'd all signed up for that possibility. But not some freak accident.

That anger, grief and skepticism were what sent him out into the scorching desert looking for the same kind of fight he'd found tonight. Something to silence the racing thoughts and numb the pain he didn't want to deal with. He'd gotten a distraction, all right. And several good men had been pulled straight into hell with him.

He never should have watched the national news story his mama had saved. The latest in a long line of shouldn'ts.

Who knew she could operate the DVR? When he left for basic training twelve years ago she could barely get a DVD to play. He'd been looking for something mindless, like old football games or episodes of *CSI.* Instead, he'd found hours of news stories detailing his capture and high-profile rescue from Taliban insurgents.

The worst had been the leaked propaganda videos. The close-up shots of his own dirt- and blood-streaked face as they'd forced him to deliver their messages to the U.S. government. He could still taste the bitter words, hated himself for saying them even if he'd done it to save Tanner from more torture he wasn't strong enough to survive.

He'd wanted to turn them off. Should have. But couldn't. What those slick news anchors with their perfect white teeth hadn't said was that what happened was entirely his fault.

His thumbs began to throb where his missing nails should have been. Gage clenched his fists tighter, asking for more. He relished the pain. The reminder. His injuries were nothing compared to Tanner's. If he hadn't let grief and a mindless need for a distraction blind him to the warning signs...

If he hadn't taken unnecessary risks and pushed them all straight into a trap, his buddy wouldn't be lying in a hospital bed looking at months of rehab, learning to live without a limb and the possibility that his military career was over.

The guy in front of him, clearly some gym rat trying to show off the muscles he'd honed in air-conditioned luxury, twisted on his heel and threw out a leg aimed straight for Gage's head. He easily blocked the kick, letting the other guy's foot glance off a shoulder.

He could wipe the floor with this guy. It had taken Gage less than ninety seconds to pick up on his weaknesses, and if they'd been in the middle of the desert instead of a crude ring made from worn padding, plywood and rope, he wouldn't have hesitated. But he wasn't there to defend his life or a set of ideals he wasn't even sure he believed anymore.

He was just there to forget. And the quickest way to that was to let this guy beat the crap out of him so he could concentrate on something other than pointless regrets and decisions he couldn't take back. Besides, he didn't need the prize money these guys were after. Better to let some struggling father win the pot so he could buy something nice for his family.

Gage's lip split. Blood splattered across the floor. His head wrenched sideways and something in the audience caught his eye. The familiar flash of green-gold eyes and dark blond hair he hadn't seen in twelve years.

Well, unless you counted dreams. And he didn't.

Hope Rawlings. His belly tightened, a sensation that had nothing to do with the repeated blows he'd taken.

Gage twisted, skillfully maneuvering his opponent so he could scour the faces surrounding them. But whatever he'd seen was gone.

Or maybe he was imagining things. Was it crazy that he would think of *her* now that he was back?

Given their history, yes, it probably was. Although, while he was reviewing regrets...

In that single moment of distraction the force of Gym Rat's fist exploded across Gage's left cheekbone. The pain reverberated through his entire face. The crunch of bone on bone burst in his ears.

"Shit." He spat out with a mouthful of blood. Well, the guy had gotten his attention again. With a sigh, Gage resigned himself to a good tongue-lashing when his mama saw him at breakfast in the morning. And decided there was no way he was letting this guy win. The next guy could take the purse.

HOPE RAWLINGS WATCHED Gage get the crap beat out of him. For fun. She tried to stay dispassionate about it. After all, it wasn't a new occurrence for him. Well, this underground, full-contact fighting for money was—maybe she could turn this into an exposé on men shedding their suits in an attempt to connect with their inner caveman—but not his penchant for finding trouble.

If they awarded medals for that... Instead, he had the Bronze Star, Prisoner of War Medal and Purple Heart. Just the thought of what he'd gone through to get those made her chest ache. And her head swell to the point of explosion. She fought against the urge to climb into that ring, snatch him by the ear and drag his ass out. Hadn't he given them all enough heart palpitations recently?

But that wasn't her place. Not anymore.

Years ago she would have been right beside him, turning blue in the face as she unsuccessfully attempted to talk him out of whatever dangerous scheme he'd hatched. They'd been friends since Gage stole her sippy cup and hit her over the head with it. They were neighbors. Their parents were best friends. *They* were best friends. Or had been. Once.

He'd been home for a couple days and was already jonesing for a hit of adrenaline. It had taken a long time for Hope to learn that she'd end up the only one hurt by hitting her head against that brick wall. Gage did what he wanted and always had. Screw anyone who stood in his way or challenged him.

That didn't make watching the smackdown any easier. Especially knowing the physical hell he'd just been through. When, exactly, would he finally say uncle? When would he have enough?

Although *watching* Gage was far from a hardship. They might have been friends, but she wasn't blind. Even as a teenager he'd been gorgeous, and knew it. Girls, attracted by the pretty face and edge of danger, had thrown themselves at him. She'd been right there beside him, dismissed by the ones who bothered to notice she was even there.

The familiar spurt of jealousy came out of nowhere. Hope pushed it down. She hadn't liked the reaction then and she definitely didn't like it now.

Wearing nothing but a pair of gym shorts, everything he had was on display. War might have left him with scars—visible and unseen—but it had definitely honed his body into something beautiful. The way he moved should have been a sin, all smooth grace and deadly calculation.

The guy he was fighting was an idiot if he couldn't see the way Gage sized him up. His stomach muscles bunched as he went on the attack. Shoulders and biceps strained. He maneuvered the other guy into a corner, limiting his opponent's range of motion. His thighs and calves flexed with every step.

Hope tried not to notice, but it was hard to tear her gaze away.

Gage was vibrant. Alive. Electric. Just being close to him always left her with the same warm buzz, like a contact high. And yet, it scared the hell out of her, too. He attacked everything so hard—life, love, danger, war. That kind of intensity was intimidating and draining for anyone standing in the fallout zone.

Dammit, when would this match end?

She wasn't here to ogle him or reminisce. She was here to interview him. He'd been avoiding her ever since he got home two days ago. Hope tried not to take it personally—he was avoiding everyone. But it still hurt.

Although, considering the things they'd both said the last time they'd spoken…she wasn't surprised. If it wasn't for the phone call she'd received three days ago she might have been avoiding him, as well. But she couldn't.

Gage Harper was her ticket out of Sweetheart.

"You want a permanent position with us, Ms. Rawlings?" Mr. Rebman had asked. He was the managing editor for the *Atlanta Courier,* a gruff man who'd only spoken to her once before for about sixty seconds—the length of time it took him to say her experience managing the *Sweetheart Sentinel* for her father did not make her a journalist. He was a real winner, but the man had the power to grant her every wish.

She'd practically tripped over her own tongue answering, "Yes, sir."

"I understand that Gage Harper is from your hometown."

And immediately Hope's stomach had seethed with sickness.

Somehow she'd found herself answering, "Yes." At least she hadn't told the man that they'd grown up together.

"He's refusing all interview offers. If you can get me an exclusive, I'll consider finding a place for you here."

Hope frowned as Gage landed another punch. So here she was, in the middle of backwoods South Carolina on a Thursday night, stalking Gage.

That sick feeling was back in the pit of her stomach.

With a sigh, Hope melted into the back of the crowd. In her four-inch heels—out of place amid the roughed-up cowboy boots—she could still see the ring just fine. Enough to know Gage had stopped playing cat and mouse and was finally going in for the kill. His opponent, a guy who never stood a chance, dropped to the floor with a groan and stayed there.

Gage bounced on his heels away from the guy, staying alert for any sign of deceit. As the nice man who'd spilled beer on her jeans had explained, there weren't any rules so dirty fighting was more than allowed. But the guy stayed down. Some in the crowd cheered and some booed.

An older guy who looked to be in charge jumped into the ring. He announced Gage as the winner, using his loud voice instead of a PA system to combat the crowd. Hope got the impression this was a traveling circus and that kind of equipment would have been a little too expensive to abandon if the cops showed up.

The guy at the door, probably a recent graduate from a halfway house, only let her in after she told him she was with one of the fighters and pointed out Gage. Even then, the way he'd eyed her with skepticism made her uncomfortable.

The crowd shifted. Someone called out demanding another fight. And with a smile and a nod of his head, the guy in charge waved the next fighter into the ring with Gage. Apparently, this wasn't the kind of place that worked off brackets. No winner-against-winner here, Gage was going again.

Hope groaned and closed her eyes, but she couldn't keep them that way for long. Not with the sound of flesh on flesh ringing in her ears again. Her overactive imagination was far worse than watching the beating. She cracked one eyelid.

Like before, Gage played with the guy for a few minutes, sizing him up. He took a few shots and gave a few back. It was clear, at least to her, that Gage had his opponent's number. So it surprised her when he left himself wide open for an uppercut beneath the chin. His back hit the floor with a resounding crack.

A man close to her groaned. He passed a handful of bills across to another guy wearing a gleeful grin. Gage didn't move. The crowd was thick enough that she couldn't tell if he was unconscious or just stunned.

Her heart fluttered uncomfortably in her chest, an echo of the panic she'd felt when news of his capture had come into the newsroom just a couple weeks before.

Here she'd thought his rescue would cure her of the unwanted reaction. Apparently not.

Hope fought against the mass of people, trying to get closer to the side of the ring. The breath she hadn't realized she was holding leaked slowly from her parted lips when he finally started to stir. His hands spread wide on the floor and he pushed upward. His head hung between those straining shoulders, as if it were too heavy for him to hold up.

Her gaze searched him for signs of serious injury. She jostled the handful of men standing between her and the ring. She yelled, demanding they let her through, and slapped at the ones who didn't listen.

Gage finally picked up his head. His gaze connected with hers through the flimsy barrier of ropes. The same punch she always felt hit her, as if she'd been the one taking shots to the solar plexus. But just like always, she ignored it.

Blood trickled from the corner of his mouth. His right eye was already swelling and bruising. Hope's hands curled around the edge of the ring floor. The sharp pain of a splinter pierced her left palm.

His golden-brown eyes flared with recognition and something warmer before narrowing down to indecipherable slits. He frowned and asked gruffly, "What are you doing here?"

"Looking for you."

In one lithe movement that belied the fact that he'd just been knocked silly, Gage bounded up from the floor and over the ropes. His feet slapped the dirty cement beside her. Several men around them smacked his back and shoulders, offering encouragement he obviously didn't need.

The man deserved an Academy Award to go with his other decorations. "You threw the match," Hope breathed out, the realization hitting at about the same time the shocked words fell from her lips. Why the heck would he do that?

His frown deepened. A few people around them stared and grumbled ominously. Gage grasped her arm and pushed her ahead of him through the crowd.

People parted to let them pass. She glanced back to look at Gage because they sure weren't moving out of *her* way. They hadn't done it any other time she'd slipped through the rowdy crowd. After seeing his expression she had to admit she didn't blame them. If he'd raked her with that hard, cutting expression she'd have gotten the hell out of the way, too.

And if he hadn't had a death grip on her upper arm she might have done it now.

Her heel caught on a crack in the floor. Before she could stumble Gage was there, keeping her from twisting an ankle by pulling her back against the wall of his chest.

His hard, sweaty chest. A shiver rocked through Hope. She just hoped he was too preoccupied to notice.

Dumping her out into the chilly February night, he finally let her go. This time she did stumble, letting the building catch her. The metal siding rattled. In the distance a peal of female laughter was cut short.

Gage stood in front of her, his legs planted wide, arms crossed over his chest. Unruly dark brown hair, longer than she'd expected, fluttered in a gust of wind. Hope shivered again, but this time it was because seeing him standing out in nothing but a pair of shorts made her cold. Spring was definitely on the way, but it was still close to forty this late at night. It didn't seem to bother him. Which bothered her.

He pinned her in place with the glittering intensity of his stare. That was new. And she wasn't sure she liked it. Where was the laughing, mischievous boy she remembered? The one whose favorite pastime was talking her into things that inevitably got them both in trouble?

Hope gathered herself, crossed her own arms to fight the sudden feeling of being exposed and stared right back.

Gage Harper might be able to intimidate a lot of people, but not her. She knew his darkest secrets—at least the ones from his childhood. She'd seen him cry when his dog was hit by a car. And she knew exactly how to get under his skin.

She didn't think he'd changed that much in twelve years. So she waited, knowing that saying nothing would eventually drive him crazy. If there was one thing Gage hated, it was silence. He needed action, movement, motion.

It only took a couple minutes for him to ask, "Why?"

"Hello to you, too, Gage. It's nice to see you home. Yeah, my daddy's doing fine, thanks for askin'. The cancer scare was difficult, but he's in remission now," she answered in the sweetest, kill-you-with-kindness voice she could manage.

He ignored her point and breezed right over the niceties. "Why were you looking for me? And for God's sake, why here? Do you know how dangerous this place is? Half the guys here are ex-cons and the other half just haven't gotten caught yet."

He was exaggerating. So none of the men inside would be up for Teddy Bear of the Year, but some of them had looked decent enough. She might have felt out of place, but not in danger.

"Please. I'm a journalist. I can handle myself."

Gage laughed. The sound wasn't what she remembered—his laugh had been loud and deep—but was brittle, with a sharp edge that could have sliced straight through skin. "You are not a journalist."

Hope jerked at the punch of his words. They shouldn't have mattered. Who cared what Gage thought? But they did. Probably because he, more than anyone, should have understood how much they would hurt. And maybe he did.

"Running Daddy's paper hardly qualifies you as a journalist. I've been home for two days and haven't seen your name on a byline yet."

Hope tried to rein in the temper she could feel bubbling inside her.

"Does my degree from Clemson make me a journalist, then?" she growled.

The minute the words left her mouth she regretted them. She watched as the expression on his face shut down, his eyes going completely blank. He took a single step backward. He didn't move far, but she realized there was more to the distance than merely putting inches between them.

He'd wounded her on purpose, but she'd done it accidentally. She should have known better. Not getting into Clemson was a sore spot for him. With that single statement she'd brought them straight back around to a history neither of them wanted to rehash.

"What do you want, Hope?"

Even his voice was distant.

"To interview you," she said, unsure how to reverse what she'd carelessly done. She could feel the opportunity to tell his story slipping through her fingers. It frustrated her.

His gaze swept across her. The contempt that grazed her made her want to walk away, but she wouldn't. She couldn't.

"I'm not giving interviews."

Even before Gage had shown up in Sweetheart, the reporters had begun crawling out of the woodwork. Several national news teams had taken up residence at the local B and B and their satellite-equipped trucks were permanently parked on every corner of the town square.

The propaganda videos released by the insurgents had made Gage Harper an overnight media sensation. The camera loved every dirty, bloody, defiant inch of his beautifully distant face. The same cuttingly intense expression filling his golden eyes had captured a nation.

And then he and his men had been rescued. Not since Jessica Lynch had there been such a media storm surrounding the capture and rescue of a U.S. soldier.

Just about every citizen of Sweetheart had been stopped and questioned about Gage—his childhood, his parents, his sister. They'd even interviewed elementary school kids who hadn't been born when Gage left and never met the guy. But in the absence of a real story, they were trying to fill in with whatever they could get their grubby hands on.

Didn't he realize that saying nothing could be worse? People filled in the blanks, anyway, with whatever they were given—whether it was fact or fiction.

The influx of reporters had become a nuisance and the town council had even called an emergency session to discuss how to deal with them. They'd hoped when

Gage came home and spoke that would be the end of it. But Gage refused to talk to anyone.

Hope had thought she—and the *Sweetheart Sentinel*—would be the exception to Gage's no-comment policy. Apparently not.

"But this is for us, Gage. Everyone wants to hear the story from you."

"Well, then I guess everyone's going to be disappointed. Something the citizens of Sweetheart should be used to where I'm concerned. I've been disappointing them for years."

"That's not true."

Gage raised a single eyebrow. It was all he needed to call her a liar, although she would have argued that *terrorized* would have been a better word than *disappointed*. Pranks like rolling the wedding gazebo, putting potato flakes in the flower beds lining Main Street so they puffed up with the morning dew and numbering three goats *1, 2* and *4* before releasing them into the high school had earned Gage a reputation.

But that was before he became a war hero.

"I'm not talking to you or anyone else, Hope."

She opened her mouth to protest, but before she could say anything he just shook his head. And began walking backward, away from her.

Hope could tell that he was determined. A lot had changed, but she'd seen that expression on his face enough times to recognize it. Every time she'd tried to talk him out of some hare-brained scheme.

However, she could be just as stubborn as he was.

She wasn't going to let anything stand between her and her escape hatch out of this town.

Not even Gage Harper. Maybe especially not Gage Harper.

2

THE TOWN WAS CRAZY. That was all there was to it. All around him chaos reigned. Although, this shouldn't have come as a surprise since he'd grown up in Sweetheart, where Valentine's Day was sacred, and folks started celebrating a week in advance. Twelve years away had managed to blunt Gage's memories.

He now recalled why he never visited at this time of year.

A group of men, most of them town-council members, were yelling at each other from the top of several ladders. "No, yours needs to go down on the right, Hank."

"I said up, Billy! You got cotton stuck in your ears again?"

Gage had mixed emotions when it came to the red banners with the white-and-pink cupids being hung on all the lampposts down Main. As a child, he'd thought the cupids looked like big blobs of cotton candy. His daddy, the mayor, had not been amused when at six he announced his opinion at the dinner table with the entire council present...and started a heated discussion about the need to update town decorations.

On the other hand, he'd used the excitement surrounding this week to snag more than one kiss beneath those banners. And why did that thought bring up an image of Hope Rawlings? She'd definitely never been one of those girls. Not that he hadn't wanted her to be....

"Gage, great to have you home," Billy Carstairs yelled as he passed between two of the men. "Boy, what happened to your face? That's not from...what happened, is it?"

As Billy looked down at him from ten feet in the air, his grip on the lamppost slipped. The banner he was holding swung precariously and Billy wobbled. The sight of him grasping the post, his cheek pressed so tightly against the metal that he vaguely resembled a smushed bulldog, might have been amusing if Gage hadn't been worried he was about to have to catch the man—all two hundred and fifty pounds of him.

"No, sir," he answered, sighing in relief when Billy regained his balance.

All around him people turned, not to watch the averted disaster, but to look at *him*. It was a sensation Gage just couldn't get used to. His neck permanently crawled from being watched. He was only a few weeks removed from an environment where that feeling usually heralded a burst of flying bullets. He'd learned to listen to those internal warnings that told him danger was coming so that he could prepare.

In Sweetheart danger tended to involve overprotective daddies with shotguns, women with wedding bells and babies on the brain and a potential shortage of beer on Saturdays during college football season. Now that could start a nasty riot.

Just one more thing he'd had to adjust to upon returning stateside.

Everyone he passed smiled and greeted him by name. Half the people he didn't even think he knew. Pride shone out of every pair of eyes. A far cry from the frowns that had followed in his wake during his teenage years.

The men probably hoped he'd stop to chat. Maybe offer a hand so they could casually ask him the question everyone wanted to know. *What happened?* Every single one of them wanted details. Or thought they did. What they really wanted was some romanticized view of what he'd been through. The drama. The rescue. The Hollywood version where everyone survived and no one had permanent scars. They didn't want the truth.

Which was fine with him since he wasn't willing to give anyone that. Although he had to admit this pedestal they'd set him up on chafed. It was lonely up here with nothing but his guilt for company.

He had no idea where he was going, but he'd needed out of the house before his mama made that disappointed, exasperated sound in the back of her throat one more time. She'd taken one look at his face and shaken her head, working out her frustration on the waffle batter she'd whipped up just for him.

Gage almost wished she'd yelled at him the way she would have when he was younger. At least then he could have gotten it over with and moved on. Instead, she went straight from the waffles to scrambled eggs and then French toast, all the while making that damned noise. He hadn't eaten this much breakfast since basic training when he'd been burning calories faster than he could shovel them in.

The sign for his sister's sweet shop, Sugar & Spice, loomed ahead. Maybe he'd stop in and see her. Although, Lexi was just as likely to chastise him and try to feed him as their mother was. But at least it gave him a purpose. He wasn't used to twiddling his thumbs while everyone else around him worked.

A bell tinkled when he opened the door. The scent of chocolate assailed him as his sister called, "Be right out."

"Take your time, Lex," he hollered back, letting her know it was only him and not a customer.

He was perusing the baked goods, truffles, fudge and caramel apples lined up neatly behind the long glass counter when the bell chimed again. Gage glanced up at the young guy who entered. He didn't look familiar, but then judging by his age, if he was local he probably would've been thirteen or fourteen when Gage left so that shouldn't surprise him.

Everyone had changed. Including his sister who was coming out of the back, wiping her hands on a red-and-white-checkered towel tucked into the waistband of her matching apron. He'd seen her over the years so her gradual growth into the beautiful woman before him hadn't completely blindsided him. But it had been at least a year since he'd last seen her. Her hair was longer. Maybe a little lighter. She'd lost another few pounds, something he didn't think she'd needed to do, but convincing Lexi of that was like talking to one of the lampposts outside.

"Gage," she said, smiling and rushing around the counter to give him a huge hug. She was always like that, exuberant and affectionate with the people who mattered to her. Sometimes he worried about that. She left herself so wide-open.... But she was a big girl and had managed fine without his meddling for a while now.

Pulling back, she held him at arm's length. A frown pulled at the edges of her wide mouth. Growing up she'd been all big eyes and mouth, both features overwhelming even her slightly pudgy face. Now she'd grown into the features, giving her an edge of uniqueness. She'd never be classified as typically beautiful, but in his mind she was better—even if he was slightly biased.

"You're here two days and you've already found trouble. I shouldn't be surprised, but I would have thought you'd had enough of that for a little while."

Gage grasped one of her bouncy curls and tugged. Her hand shot to her scalp as her head tilted into the torture. But she was laughing as she said, "Ow, don't make me tell Mom."

"Oh, she knows. I got waffles, scrambled eggs, pumpkin muffins and French toast as punishment."

Lexi scowled. "How the heck is that punishment? Sounds like she did everything but kill the fatted calf."

"Don't worry, that's for dinner tonight. Please say you're coming because if I have to endure any more of the fawning I think I'm going to scream."

Lexi had moved out of their parents' house years ago into a cute little cottage on the lake. Because this was one of her busiest seasons, he'd only seen her briefly his first night home. Gage definitely could have used her as a buffer against their mother's ebullient praise and their father's silent, watchful gaze. He almost wished his dad would say something already—like how he'd screwed up once again.

"It'll cost you," she said, grinning evilly, spinning away from him to the customer waiting patiently at the other end of the counter. "Head into the back. I'll be there in a few. What can I get for you today? Are you shopping for someone special?"

"What are these?" The guy pointed to some fancy chocolates set apart from the rest of the displays. Gage bit back a smile, listening with half an ear as his sister launched into a lecture about the herb-laced aphrodisiac chocolates she specialized in.

Shaking his head, Gage slipped behind the red curtain that separated the industrial kitchen and office space from the main display area. Up front the store was all quaint ambience. Iron scrollwork chairs and polished tea tables. Hand-carved wood-and-glass display cases. She'd even gone so far as to distress the pieces to make them look antique and give the place an artificial air of history. Behind the curtain was the land of efficient stainless steel.

She'd been open for about six years, and according to his parents was doing very well. A few years ago she started selling some of the more exotic concoctions on the internet. He was glad.

The low rumble of a male voice and the lilting sound of his sister's laughter drifted back to him. One minute stretched into five. And then ten. Gage wandered the kitchen, tempted to open the doors to the double oven to determine what smelled so damn good. But he didn't. He'd been chased away with a wooden spoon often enough to know better.

Instead, he grabbed a spoon and dipped it into a large bowl of melted chocolate. Closing his eyes, he breathed, "Heaven." It had been a very long time since he'd tasted something so good. Gourmet chocolate wasn't exactly normal fare in the mess hall.

Finally, Lexi slid through the curtain. She shot forward, smacking his spoon away just as he was going in for another taste. "That's a food safety violation, you idiot. I'll have to throw the whole batch away if you put that spoon back in."

"No one will know. I won't tell if you don't." Lexi glared at him, but there was no heat behind the empty gesture.

"Who was that guy?" Gage asked, using the spoon he'd licked clean to point up front.

Lexi shrugged, but he didn't miss the faint pink that stained her cheeks. "Tourist in for the week."

Oh, no. He knew that look on his sister's face. From twelve to twenty-six it hadn't changed. She was terrible at hiding her thoughts—or her interest in the opposite sex. "Men don't usually come to Sweetheart for Valentine's week alone, Lex." He tapped the end of her nose with the edge of his spoon. "Don't let this week go to your head."

Her eyes, as dark as the chocolate he'd just tasted, dulled and she frowned. "Like I could."

"What's that supposed to mean?" Gage asked.

"Nothing." Lexi waved her comment away, the short spurt of sadness disappearing almost as quickly as it had come up. "So Mama's seen the shiner...has Daddy?"

She crossed over to the long line of work counters, pulling out a tray of the biggest strawberries he'd ever seen, and began dipping them into the vat of melted chocolate. She placed them on a waxed paper–covered tray and then drizzled white chocolate and a thin strand of caramel across the surface. Gage's mouth began to water.

"Uh...no," he said, scooting closer to better position himself for a sneak attack.

She eyed him and without even breaking the routine of dip-and-drizzle repositioned her body as a barrier between him and those strawberries. "You gonna tell me what happened?" she asked, picking up the first berry and handing it to him. "Be careful, it's still wet. Consider that a bribe to leave the rest of my inventory alone. I'm worried I'll be short this week as it is."

Gage took a huge bite of the strawberry, the perfect combination of tart and sweet. It was also the perfect excuse not to answer her question. Telling her what he'd been doing would lead to *why* he'd been doing it, and he just didn't want to go there. Especially with his baby sister.

Instead, he chose to distract her with a less revealing confession. "I've been home two days and I'm already bored out of my mind. I'm not used to an entire day with no purpose. I need to...do something."

"And you thought going to Baxter to fight in some underground ring would help?"

Gage nearly choked. "How do you know about that?"

"Hope is one of my best friends." It was Lexi's turn to pop him with the back of a spoon. "You don't think she'd mention seeing you at a place like that?"

He hadn't realized Hope had become that close with his sister. Growing up, it had been he and Hope who'd been inseparable. And although they hadn't talked in years, he wasn't sure he liked the idea of Hope being so chummy with Lexi.

Lexi dropped the last berry onto the tray. "What

the hell were you thinkin'? You shouldn't have walked off and left her there, Gage. She could have gotten into some serious trouble."

She wasn't saying anything Gage hadn't already thought. He'd been halfway home on his dad's vintage Harley before his temper had cooled enough that his brain kicked in. When would he learn to stop and think before erupting?

He'd turned around and gone back to look for her, but she'd already left.

It was nice to know she'd gotten home okay, though. One weight out of many he could let drop from his shoulders.

"She never should have been there, Lex."

The punch of anger and disappointment he'd felt last night when he'd realized why Hope had followed him resurfaced.

He called himself ten different kinds of fool for the brief spurt of excitement and anticipation when he'd seen her. You'd think being told you were an idiot with a death wish and having your declaration of feelings thrown back in your face would have killed any desire to have her.

Apparently not.

Even now he could remember that last night, twelve years ago. They'd been at the gazebo. It had been late, close to midnight, the town long past quiet and asleep. But he was wired from enlisting, excited about the possibilities of the life he was about to start, and hadn't been able to sleep. He'd called her and asked her to meet him.

Watching her walk down the aisle surrounded by the ghost of empty chairs had galvanized something inside him. Suddenly he wanted—*needed*—her with him on the adventure he was about to start. Hope had always been there for him, with an eye roll, rebuke or encouragement depending on what the situation needed. When he'd screwed up and lost his scholarship to Clemson, and couldn't escape his dad's wrath, she'd been there to tell him everything would be fine. She had faith in him when no one else, including himself, did.

But when he'd needed her the most she'd completely flaked on him. He could still see her wild-eyed reaction to his confession that he loved her. He hadn't meant to tell her, it had just slipped out.

Part of him had always known she'd reject him. He must have asked her out a hundred times, but the answer was always the same. The first time they'd probably been eight or nine and it had quickly become a running joke between them. He'd ask her out in the most ridiculous, cheesy ways possible. And she'd always say no.

Even he wasn't exactly sure when it stopped being funny and started being real. But Hope hadn't noticed the difference and he'd been too much of a coward to make her see.

Even back then everyone thought he was so strong. Her rejection had been the one thing that scared the hell out of him.

She'd been so angry with him that night. Upset that he'd enlisted. Angry that he'd done it without talking to her about the decision. And when he'd wrapped his arms around her and told her he loved her she'd pushed him away.

Exactly what he'd always feared. But he'd survived her rejection and a heck of a lot worse since then. His thumbs throbbed dully as if he needed the reminder.

Why was he reliving the memory? Probably because seeing her last night, being in this place especially around Valentine's Day, brought everything rushing back.

It shouldn't bother him that she'd followed him to that fight with ulterior motives, but it did. "She came looking for a story, just like all the other buzzards circling around this place." He despised the bitterness in his own voice.

"Not like all the others. Hope is a friend, Gage. The two of you used to be real close. If you're going to talk to anyone, it should be her. Hope is family."

He snorted. "She's far from that."

Lexi frowned at him, narrowing her eyes. "I have no idea what happened between you two, and I don't wanna know, but nothing she could have done makes leaving her in a place like that okay."

With a sigh, Lexi switched the subject. "Since you're so bored, I'm sure Mama would be happy to find you a job. Cupid's Couples starts tonight with the matching. Did you put your name in?"

"Hell, no." The last thing Gage needed was a week full of candy hearts, wilted flowers and awkward dinners with a stranger. And even if he had grown up with most of the single women in the town, after twelve years away they were all strangers. "I just escaped one hell, why would I sign up for another?"

"Didn't you hear? They're donating all the money raised to the Wounded Warrior Project in honor of your friend Tanner."

"Well, fu—" Lexi glared at him "—dge." He'd planned to ignore the whole damn thing. Stay at home and refuse to attend. But now, there was no way he could blow the events off. Showing up was the least he could do for Tanner.

Before he could ask Lexi for suggestions on how he might help, the front bell rang again. And again. And again. Feet shuffled against the polished floor. Several voices rang out, "Hello!" and someone slammed a palm down onto the display case, rattling the glass countertop.

"What the hell," Lexi grumbled.

In full-on big-brother mode, Gage followed quickly behind her, but didn't get farther than the curtain before Lexi slapped her hands onto his chest and pushed him backward.

"Get back. Get back," she ordered, her eyes full of fire.

Gage caught enough of a glimpse to recognize the horde of reporters who now filled Lexi's store. Jostling for position at the counter, they held high-powered cameras with special lenses, pens poised above notepads and video cameras with blinking red lights.

Damn, he hated the media.

He really wished one of the other guys would get released from the hospital. Not just because he needed them to be okay, but because then maybe some of these vultures would start circling *their* lives for the details about the capture and rescue.

He let his sister shove him deeper into the kitchen. "You can slip out the back door. Take the alley," she suggested.

Considering the alternative, that was exactly what he was going to do. "Make 'em buy something. The most expensive item you have in the store. And then tell them I'm staying at the old Jones place out by the lake. It's still empty, right?"

"Yeah."

The place had been abandoned for as long as he could remember, but it was on the far side of the lake on the outskirts of town, which meant he'd have at least an hour of peace before they realized Lexi's lie and headed back.

Unfortunately, he had to walk straight across Main in order to get back to his parents' house. Which meant he needed to find some place to lay low until the plague was gone.

Gage glanced up and down the alley. The bridal salon was two doors down from Sugar & Spice, but the thought of going in there made those cameras look almost appealing. Scent of Woman might have been an option, Lanie's mother had always loved him, but he really didn't want to smell like a flower the rest of the day. Which also left Petals, the florist, out.

His eyes skipped across the back door to the *Sweetheart Sentinel,* and then jerked back again. The newspaper. Probably the last place the journalists he was trying to escape would look for him. So the first place he should hide. It had been a long time since he'd seen Mr. Rawlings, although he wasn't sure the man had ever liked him much.

But Gage was willing to take his chances.

3

DARTING DOWN THE NARROW passage, Gage grasped the back door and pulled it open. He half expected to walk into chaos—probably thanks to false Hollywood portrayals. Instead, everything was quiet. Oh, there were people working. He could hear the hushed rumble of voices, the clack of keyboards and the faint buzzing of a telephone.

He rounded the corner to a cubicle and stuck his head inside. Erica McNeil looked up from her computer screen, a startled expression on her face. "Gage Harper. What are you doing here?" Her shy gaze darted away from his. "How'd you get in?"

"Back door." He grinned and leaned against the hard metal edge of her cubicle wall.

"What happened to your face? Is that from…" Her voice trailed off, her eyes widened and a faint blush crept up her pale cheeks. Everyone either wanted all the details of his capture and torture or they wanted to pretend it hadn't happened. Apparently Erica was in the latter group.

"Nope. I ran into a door."

Her already-large eyes rounded more with surprise… and then narrowed to slits. Erica was about six or seven years older than he was and had babysat Lexi a few times. She always had been gullible.

"Stop harassing Erica."

Hope's voice sounded behind him. Gage smiled, although Erica was the only one to see it because before he spun around, he'd wiped it clean.

Adopting an air of innocence, he turned slowly to look at her. Her hands were balled into fists and lodged firmly on her hips. Her toe tapped against the worn carpeted floor, drawing his gaze down the long length of her legs. Up and down, up and down, the red sole of her black high heels flashed like a beacon.

He always had been a leg man and he had to admit Hope had a nice pair. Was it his imagination or were they even more toned than before?

Gage forced his gaze back up her body, taking in the tight skirt, silk blouse and matching suit jacket she wore. She looked like a high-powered businesswoman. Someone ready to take on the world and stomp it beneath the spiked heel of her shoe.

She was seriously overdressed for the *Sweetheart Sentinel.* He couldn't remember ever seeing Hank, her father, wearing anything that resembled a business suit. Not even a blazer when he'd been honored by the town council as citizen of the year. He wondered if anyone had told Hope that. Not that he cared.

"I wasn't harassing anyone, was I, Erica?" he asked, shooting her a disarming smile over his shoulder.

Erica's gaze swung between them. Without answering his question, she swiveled in her chair, giving them her back and returning her focus to her computer screen.

Hope eyed him. He noticed how her gaze lingered on the damage to his face. But unlike everyone else, she knew exactly how he'd gotten the injuries. And unlike everyone else, she didn't remark on them, but turned and walked away.

He followed. How could he not? The view of her tight rear was so tempting. The slit at the back of her skirt swished back and forth as she walked. It brushed against the inside of her thighs. Gage couldn't tear his eyes away. Desire, hot and hard, punched through him. He almost stumbled.

After a quick, calming breath, Gage followed her inside the office just in time to watch her sink gracefully into the chair behind a large desk. The blotter was perfectly clean. Two folders, neatly labeled, sat to her left. A matching tape dispenser, stapler and hole punch were lined up beside them along with a cup of pens and a basket of paper clips. Just like her flawless suit, there was no clutter.

He wanted to loosen her up. To unravel that elegant twist in her hair and tousle it with his fingers. To pop open a few of those tightly closed buttons so that he could see the lace camisole beneath. To scrape everything off her desk and lay her out beneath him...

Oh, crap, where had that come from?

"Are you here to give me that interview, Gage?"

Clearing his throat and tossing the unwanted fantasy away, he dropped into the chair across from her. "Hell, no." He sprawled, his long legs reaching beneath the desk to brush against the toe of her shoe.

She pulled it back. Gage's lips twitched.

"Then why are you here?"

"I'm hiding."

"From whom?"

"Does it matter?"

She studied him for several seconds before slowly saying, "Yes, I think it does."

Gage shrugged. "Some reporters tracked me into Lexi's store. I have no idea how they found me." He placed his elbows on the opposite edge and leaned halfway across her desk. She started to back away, but stopped herself. He stared straight at her, hard and deadly, just for the fun of watching her eyes flash indignantly. "Any idea how they could have known I was in there?"

Hope's mouth tightened with annoyance. "You're kidding, right? Your photograph was splashed on every news outlet for weeks. They've been camped out here since before you were rescued. Unless you walk around town with a paper bag over your head, you're doomed."

"Don't you think the paper bag would defeat the purpose? I mean, isn't that a little conspicuous?"

Hope's mouth twisted into a pitiful approximation of a smile. "Funny. And as much as I'd love to help you—" her tone of voice called that statement all kinds of liar "—we have a business to run, Gage. So unless you're here for official reasons—"

"I'm not giving you an interview."

"—you need to leave."

She stood up from her desk, tugged at the hem of her skirt to make sure it was straight and walked around to stand expectantly beside him. Gage didn't move. Instead, he turned his head and got a great view of the curve of her hip and ass. Why would he want to leave? He was perfectly happy right here.

Slowly, his eyes tracked upward. His head dropped back so he could see the tight expression on her face. Old habits died hard and he wanted to do something completely inappropriate to wipe it away. "You're going to throw me out? In my time of need?"

"You forget, I know you're about as helpless as a rat-tlesnake. And if I needed a reminder, you gave it to me last night. Out." She hitched a thumb over her shoulder toward her open doorway.

Reluctantly, Gage unfolded from the chair. But instead of going around the opposite side, he crowded into Hope's personal space. She didn't back down. He'd always admired her tenacity. It probably made her a damn good journalist. Well, it would have if she'd had the chance to sink her teeth into any stories.

Dread and anticipation coiled through him as he realized *he* was the story she'd decided to sink into. A vision of her pert mouth stretched wide as her sharp teeth dug into his naked hip almost made him groan.

He wanted to grab her, to pull her into him and kiss her until he forgot everything but the feel of her mouth. It wasn't a new desire, although he hadn't felt it in a very long time. How inconvenient for it to suddenly resurface.

She must have realized something had changed because she stepped back. Her spine pressed into the wall. Her palms flattened against the uninteresting tan surface. The drab background only served to emphasize the stark contrast of her pink-tinged skin and watchful, wary green-gold eyes.

She drew in a deep breath, her breasts rising against

the tight confines of her jacket. She held it for several seconds before blowing it slowly out again. That kind of control had always fascinated Gage. Hope was so… contained.

She didn't need anything or anyone. When they were younger he'd thought of himself as the one exception to that rule. It had always made him feel special, especially when he couldn't seem to do anything else right. But, as it turned out, she'd been able to cut him out of her life with little fuss.

He closed the space between them. Her body stiffened.

He didn't touch her. He didn't have to. Her scent surrounded him, something sweet with a hint of spice running underneath. Perfectly Hope. He could feel the heat of her. It warmed him in a way that even the hottest day in the middle of the desert hadn't been able to do.

Her lips parted. He didn't think it was intentional, but the motion still drew his attention.

Instead of doing what he wanted, Gage reached up and poked her straight in the ribs.

She wheezed, a sound halfway between laughter and surprise, and bent sideways away from his finger.

"What are you doing?" She slapped his hand away and he let her.

"Rumpling that perfect exterior."

"What perfect exterior?"

"The one you've expertly crafted to make people forget that you spent years loudly telling everyone just how far you were planning to get from this place. Funny, looks like you didn't get quite as far as you'd hoped."

The flash of hurt was quick and immediately covered

with narrow-eyed pique. But he saw it. And regretted that he'd caused it.

But he shouldn't. The fact that anything he said had the power to wound her was surprising. Although it didn't exactly change anything.

He moved in closer. He was tall, and as Hope was wearing heels, they were almost perfectly matched. Gage brought his mouth to the tender shell of her ear and whispered, "I know exactly who you are, Hope. Your most intimate secrets. The sound of your laughter. The smell of your favorite shampoo. How you nibbled the cap on your pen during tests. Did you know I spent years fantasizing about getting my hands on you?"

He pulled back, studying her for some reaction, although he wasn't exactly certain what. Maybe surprise. Or distaste. Or possibly even interest. He didn't find any of those things, just an alert cautiousness.

She wanted something from him. It should have felt better to be able to deny her. Just like she'd denied him so many years ago. When he'd finally gotten up the courage to tell her that all those times he'd asked her out hadn't been a joke. That he meant it every single time and had wanted her for years. And each time she'd uttered the word *no* it had wounded him just a little.

He was so close that he could see the golden flecks in her eyes. The leery burn of them. He stared straight into her and said, "Disappointment's a bitch, isn't it?"

SHE FUMED, SILENTLY, UNABLE to move away from the wall even after he'd gone. Her body shook with a combination of anger and relief.

"Was that Gage Harper I just saw leaving?"

Her dad walked into her office and plopped down into the chair Gage had just occupied.

His silver-brown hair was disheveled, as if he'd either just rolled out of bed or spent the past several hours tugging at the thinning strands. Hope wanted to think that it was the latter, but she was afraid it was the former.

Her dad had been spending less and less time at the paper in the past few years, making her life even crazier than it already was. They were a small operation, so on a good day she was CEO, bookkeeper, referee, marketing, content and traffic cop all rolled into one. Usually at once. It was amazing she didn't get brained by one of the balls she constantly juggled.

Which didn't sit well with her. She'd tried to talk to him about his lack of interest but he just changed the subject or ignored her.

She'd come home right after college, almost seven years ago, to take care of him and the paper while he recovered from cancer treatment. The surgery and the months of chemo and recovery as he regained his strength had been difficult on them both, but he had been in remission for years now.

The problem was that while his energy had returned, his interest in the *Sentinel* hadn't. She'd gently suggested he look for a buyer. But he'd gotten angry, telling her not to be silly, that it had been in their family for over a hundred years.

What was she supposed to do? Let her family's heritage crumble around her from neglect? She was stuck. The only way out involved getting a job that removed her from the equation completely and forced his hand.

"Yes," she growled, glaring at her dad.

He did a double take, finally looking at her for the first time since he'd walked into the room.

"Well, there's no reason to be snippy. I just asked a simple question."

He was right. The person she was really angry with had already fled the scene. Taking out her frustrations on her dad wouldn't help. Especially since they already had enough unresolved issues.

Taking a deep breath, Hope offered, "I'm sorry," and tried to put a smile with the words.

She must have been at least partially successful, because her dad smiled back. "No problem, pumpkin. I know you're under a lot of stress."

Okay, now the anger was pointed squarely at him. "Yes, as a matter of fact, I am. Do you know what would lessen that stress?"

"A night out?"

"No!" Hope stalked across her small office and propped her hip against the desk so she could stare straight into her dad's eyes and pin him to the spot. "You being here! That's what would help my stress level. How many times do I have to tell you that I don't want to run the paper?"

His eyebrows dropped over narrowed eyes. "I don't remember asking you to."

"You didn't have to. Who do you think the staff come to when they have a problem or question and you're not here?"

"So don't answer them, Hope. They know how to reach me when I'm off site. Don't pin your own relentless need to pick up every burden you walk past on me. Tell them no."

Hope growled low in her throat.

"Anyway, that's not why I came in here."

Needing some space, Hope slipped around her desk and sank into the waiting comfort of her chair. She wasn't up for having this argument—again—today. Not after her encounter with Gage. Nothing she said ever changed the outcome, anyway.

"I was cleaning out the safety deposit box and found this." Her dad held out a burgundy velvet box. "Thought you might want to wear it to the cocktail party tomorrow night."

Slowly, Hope reached across the desk for it. Before she'd even touched it she knew the nap on the box would be soft and worn. It had been…years since she'd seen it.

The hinges creaked as she lifted the lid. Nestled against the dark red satin lining was a beautiful necklace-and-earring set. The large ruby teardrop pendant hung from a delicate gold chain. The links gleamed with age and care. The earrings were smaller ruby teardrops with diamond chips at the top. Both pieces were heirlooms and had been given to her mother by her father's grandmother when her parents had gotten married.

The last memory Hope had of the set was when she'd been eight—no, maybe nine—and watched as her parents prepared for the Cupid's Couples charity party. She'd wanted desperately to go, but they'd told her she was too young.

Later that month her mom had died in a car crash.

The familiar pain lanced through her. It had been over twenty years. She wondered when the loss would stop sneaking up on her.

"I thought you'd sold these," she breathed softly.

"Why would I do that?" her dad asked, incredulously.

She shrugged. "I don't know. You've just never mentioned them so I assumed you didn't have them anymore."

"Your mom liked me to keep it in the safety deposit box when she wasn't wearing it. I decided to leave it there until you got older and I could give it to you. Your mom wanted you to have it on your wedding day."

Her wedding day? Even the mention of it gave her heart palpitations. "Whoa, I'm not even dating anyone."

Her dad gave her a tiny frown. "I know. But I wanted to see you wear them and thought this was the perfect occasion. I know you're going to the party. Maybe they'll be a good luck charm and you'll catch some nice man's eye."

"Dad, I do not need a man."

Her dad was buying in to the town propaganda just a little too much for her peace of mind. Sure, Sweetheart embraced the hearts-and-flowers thing with gusto. The image pulled in tourists from nearby Charleston and Hilton Head and had provided them a sustaining source of income when the textile mill outside of town shut down more than twenty years ago.

The town was the perfect setting already, providing a charming, small-town romantic escape for couples and honeymooners. The Cupid's Couples events had been going on for over fifty years.

But this was reality and her life in particular they were talking about. Marriage wasn't part of her plan, at least not until her journalism career was back on track, which wasn't going to happen as long as she was stuck at the *Sentinel*.

"You're putting your name in for Cupid's Couples at least, right?"

Hope sighed. She could lie to her dad... "I hadn't planned on it."

"Why ever not, Hope? Your mom would be disappointed in you."

She sucked in another breath against the surprise. How could she argue with him? She had no idea if her mom would be disappointed or not. She'd been too young when she died to really know her. She'd only seen her through the eyes of a child, not an adult aware of more than just her own selfish desires.

They were talking an awful lot about her mom today. Hope couldn't remember the last time her dad had mentioned her... Probably not since his own illness and recovery.

That entire experience had been difficult for her—the prospect of losing her only remaining parent. Even now the thought sent panic skittering just beneath her skin. Wanting to change the subject, Hope returned to something that had been bothering her since he'd said it. "Why were you cleaning out the safety deposit box?"

He glanced away from her, suddenly finding something incredibly interesting on the wall behind her head. "No reason, really. It was a chore I've been putting off for a while. It's so easy to forget what's in there."

Leaning across the desk, Hope grasped her dad's hand. His startled eyes shot to hers.

"Is everything okay?" she asked.

"Yes," he answered without flinching.

"Thank you for Mom's jewelry. I'll wear it tomorrow."

Happiness stretched across his face. "Wonderful." Pulling his hand out from under hers, her dad stood and headed for the door.

He turned, and with that mischievous glint in his eyes that always left her feeling slightly uneasy, he said, "Maybe you can use their glitter to catch Gage's eye. He's always had a thing for you and it would be a coup for our little paper if you could get an exclusive interview."

Yeah. She'd get right on that. And worry later about disappointing her dad by giving the story to the *Courier*.

4

HOPE WAS ALWAYS AMAZED at the Cupid committee's ability to completely transform the basement of St. Luke's. For as long as she could remember the cocktail party that kicked off the weeklong festivities had been held at the church. Tonight everyone who had paid to be paired—and a few who hadn't—would be matched with an eligible man or woman for Valentine's week. They'd participate in events and go out on dates. The hope being that after the week some of the couples might find they were perfect together. Hope had other plans for the man she'd nominated and the week she'd purchased.

Apparently the theme this year was red and gold. Someone had tacked large panels of dark red crushed velvet along the walls, camouflaging the peeling beige paint beneath. Swags of gauzy gold material hid the boring acoustic-tiled ceiling and caught the light from the hundreds of candles burning on the tables, bouncing it back onto the crush of people milling below.

Normally St. Luke's was big enough to comfortably hold the entire town, but with the addition of tourists even the huge basement was stretched to capacity. Although no one—young, old, single, taken—would miss Matching Night. Too much gossip.

One of their reporters was moving through the crowd, ready to report all the drama. Tonight she was more likely to *be* the story than the one recounting it. Not that she intended to tell anyone her role in what was about to go down.

Not if she expected it all to work… Butterflies fluttered uncomfortably inside her belly. She couldn't remember the last time she'd been nervous. Maybe college. Yeah, probably over some major exam.

And, really, this wasn't much different. When she thought about it, her reaction was normal. An assignment. A test. That's all this was. It had nothing to do with Gage or the fact that she'd pulled a sizable chunk out of her rainy day fund to ensure she had an entire week of his undivided attention.

Pressing a hand to her tummy to calm the butterflies, she stood on tiptoe and tried to find her friends.

She spotted Jenna, the town's only caterer and one of her best friends, by the large—and temporary—bar, and waved. When Jenna noticed her she mouthed "everything okay?" Jenna gave a single nod that was at odds with the frown lines creasing the middle of her forehead. But before Hope could move that way one of the tux-clad waitstaff was pulling her away.

Hope debated whether to go after her, but decided Jenna was probably just stressed and interrupting would only add to that.

"Over here," Lexi called out, waving from a table halfway across the room. Hope pushed through the crowd, slipping into the last empty seat.

Around the table their friends greeted her—Macey, Willow, Jade, Lanie, Regan and Tatum. Normally, Jenna would have been part of their group, but she was obviously busy tonight.

They were an eclectic bunch. She'd known Willow, Lanie and Jade from kindergarten, and despite a few hormone-fueled moments during their teenage years, they'd always been close. Tatum had joined their group when she moved here to buy Petals. Willow, always worried about making everyone feel welcome, had adopted her. She shouldn't have worried. Tatum could be abrasive, but you always knew where you stood with her and everyone rather liked her. Macey, a bit older than the rest of them, was Willow's business partner.

Despite the difference in their ages, Hope and Lexi had always been friends, growing up on the same street. Although, Hope had been even closer to Gage. At least until he left. After Lexi opened Sugar & Spice right behind the newspaper offices their friendship had quickly rekindled. At first Hope had worried Lexi would hold a grudge for how her friendship with Gage had ended, but she'd never even mentioned it. Hope was glad because she really liked Lexi.

"What have I missed?" Hope asked, eyeing the line at the bar and calculating whether she had time to grab a martini before the festivities started.

"Not much," Tatum groused. "No catfights yet, but I pray that ends pretty quickly."

Lexi just rolled her eyes. "You know you don't have to be here."

"And miss all the excitement?" Tatum exclaimed, her eyes round with mock innocence as she gulped down her whiskey and seven.

Tatum had grown up in Detroit and didn't always get the idiosyncrasies that came with living in a small southern town—like antiquated traditions that went back generations. But she always attended, even if she needed some liquid courage to get through the experience.

"You know, one of these years I'm going to pay to put your name in just so I can see you squirm," Lexi threatened, a gleam in her eye.

Willow leaned across the table. "This year. Please, do it this year. I need the entertainment."

"Don't worry." Tatum rattled the naked ice in her empty glass and eyed the bar line. "I brought my checkbook just in case I needed a get-out-of-jail payment. I'm not interested in any of the men in this town and I have no intention of being forced into a torturous week with one of them."

"Oh, come on, they aren't that bad. There must be someone you're interested in." Jade plucked the glass out of Tatum's hand and plopped her mostly untouched amaretto sour in its place. Tatum took a sip, grimaced, eyed the bar line again and drank some more.

"You forget. I deliver flowers to the wives when they feel guilty and the mistresses when they don't."

Hope just shook her head. Weren't florists supposed to be romantics? To have perpetual smiles and sunny dispositions? That definitely did not describe Tatum.

"What about Gage?" Macey's soft voice piped up. Lexi frowned.

"What about him?" Tatum asked.

"Well, he's a war hero. Just home, so you've never met him and definitely haven't delivered any flowers to wife, mistress or girlfriend. What's wrong with him?"

Tatum's gaze shifted to Lexi for a moment. Pain and guilt filled her eyes before flitting away. What the heck was that about? "Nothing. I'm sure he's great, but I don't do soldiers."

"Who do you do?" Regan asked.

Willow shocked them all by adding, "You know if it's girls we'd be fine with that."

Tatum sputtered, choking out, "No," as she tried to inhale her drink.

"Just checking." Willow shrugged.

Gage slipped up behind his sister, wrapping her in the kind of hug that left Lexi bent over. "Save me," he pleaded.

The butterflies took flight again inside Hope's belly.

"Can't. Breathe," Lexi wheezed out, swatting at his arms clamped around her body.

His shoulder muscles flexed against the straining seams of his jacket. He was wearing his dress uniform, although Hope almost wished he hadn't. It was…too much. He looked too good in it.

Something white flashed, drawing her eyes down to his hands and the bandages wrapped around his thumbs. Paired with the uniform they were both reminders of what he'd been through.

That he'd almost died.

A familiar temper that she thought she'd dealt with years ago punched through her. Logically, she realized she shouldn't be upset with him for serving his country. And, really, she didn't want to be. He'd made an honorable career choice.

One that had almost killed him.

Hope rolled her shoulders, and fought the urge to reach out and touch him—to make sure that he was real and there, instead of stuck in some dark hole in the middle of a hostile country.

To her, enlisting had been tantamount to Gage signing his own death warrant. She knew him too well. He was constantly pushing boundaries, testing himself and everyone around him. And it wasn't as if he'd been destined for a desk job. Oh, no, it had been the front lines or nothing for him. From the moment he'd signed up his intention had been to get that Ranger Tab. And he'd done it.

But the thought of losing someone else she cared about... Hope just couldn't do it.

Not that it had mattered any when the phone call about his capture had come into the newsroom. She hadn't talked to him in twelve years and it had still felt as if her world was suddenly spinning out of control. She couldn't concentrate on anything and didn't sleep more than a couple hours at a time until he'd been rescued.

So he was home and safe with only a few scars to show for the adventure. That status quo wouldn't keep, and Hope knew it.

The butterflies swarmed up her throat, choking her. She swallowed them back down. And jerked her gaze straight up to Gage's. He watched her, frowning.

Throwing her a dark glance, he grabbed a chair from another table and spun it close. "Gage," Lexi yelped when he picked her up, chair and all, to make room. Her embarrassed gaze darted around. "What are you doing?"

With a negligent shrug, he set her down again and insinuated himself between Hope and Lexi. "Hiding."

"Well, you suck at it," Hope said. "You stick out like a sore thumb."

Willow gasped at her unintended pun. Hope cringed inwardly and fought the urge to look at the appendage she'd inadvertently brought into the conversation. Her nose wrinkled. Gage's eyes narrowed.

Crossing his arms over that wide chest, he sprawled into his chair. Hope was worried the spindly back might give from his sheer power.

"A sore thumb, huh?"

Hope's throat went dry, but she ignored it. Nodding, she raised an eyebrow and decided to brazen it out. "I would have expected someone with your training would be better at blending in, that's all."

"What do you know about my training?" He watched her, his gaze steady and unwavering even as it bored into her.

"Enough." From the moment she'd heard Gage had been captured she'd found herself doing internet searches on everything she could find about the Rangers. She'd wanted to know just how much danger he'd been in.

The thought of him being tortured… It was one thing to realize he faced death every single day, but the kind of continued pain and suffering those white bandages represented was so much worse.

A taunting smile played at the corner of Gage's mouth, doing nothing more than tugging up the edges. He'd always had the best smile. The kind of lopsided imperfection that carried a healthy dose of roguish charm.

Hope realized she hadn't seen that smile once since he'd been home. Something tightened in the center of her chest. Absentmindedly, she reached up and rubbed the spot. Gage's gaze followed the motion, snagging on the scooped neckline of her strapless dress.

Heat flamed up her chest. Quickly, she moved her hand up to circle her throat and grabbed the pendant hanging there instead. The prongs from the setting dug into her and so did the tiny kernel of guilt for what she was about to do.

But it was too late to stop, even if she wanted to. Which she didn't.

Gage shifted beside her. The tight seam of his uniform jacket strained against his shoulders. Lexi said something to him, Hope wasn't even sure what. He turned away, releasing her from the pressure that had been building...until his arm dropped carelessly over the scalloped edge of her chair. Warm fingers brushed the curve of her naked shoulder. She nearly knocked Lanie's drink over when she jackknifed away from the contact.

Several pairs of shocked eyes—but not Gage's—turned to look at her. Luckily she was saved from coming up with an explanation when Mrs. Copeland walked to the podium in all her heirloom jewelry and big-hair glory.

A HUSH RIPPLED THROUGH the crowd. Gage suppressed the need to ruin the moment by dropping a glass to the floor or knocking one of the large floral centerpieces over. It was a childish urge and most of him realized that, but old habits died hard and troublemaker had been the only role he'd ever filled at these events until now.

To distract himself, he leaned forward, making some unnecessary comment to one of Lexi's friends just so he could brush his fingertips across the smooth surface of

Hope's skin again. A shiver rippled through her body. He felt it, relished the reaction.

Perhaps his commanding officer was right and he was a masochist. He thought he'd learned his lesson with Hope a very long time ago, but apparently not.

Although, he had always loved playing with fire. Loved the excitement, the adrenaline, the knowledge that the reward was always better when you had to battle for what you wanted.

It was gratifying to realize Hope wasn't as immune to him as she'd like.

A spotlight cut through the intentional gloom and wrapped around Mrs. Copeland.

Leaning closer to Hope, he brought his lips to her ear and whispered, "Isn't that the same dress she wore our senior year?"

She choked, making a desperate wheezing sound in the back of her throat even as she threw him a warning glare.

"Welcome to our annual Cupid's Couple festival," Mrs. Copeland began.

Everyone around him, including Hope, burst into applause. Gage didn't bother. Not only was he less than enthusiastic about the whole damn thing, but it also would have required him to move his hand and he rather liked where it was.

"For our guests who aren't familiar with our little tradition, over fifty years ago the citizens of Sweetheart decided Valentine's Day was the perfect opportunity to pair off our single young people. The first event was a modest dance, but since then it's grown into this week-long celebration."

She bestowed a benevolent smile across the entire

crowd as if she was solely responsible for this boom in attendance. And she probably thought she was. For as long as he could remember Mrs. Copeland had been running an etiquette school for young men and women.

He'd been kicked out around age thirteen. The lizard he'd put down the back of her dress had died a valiant death for a good cause. To steal a phrase from Mrs. Copeland herself, bless his squished heart.

"For the past week our town Cupid has been receiving nominations for those interested in participating in our festivities. Tonight the fun begins when each of our young ladies is paired with an escort for the week.

"While we don't expect everyone will fall madly in love…" Mrs. Copeland winked conspiratorially at the crowd. The gesture might have worked if her false eyelashes hadn't been so heavy that she could barely open her eye again. "I'll be surprised if we don't have several permanent matches after the festivities are over.

"But don't worry, there's plenty of fun even if Cupid's arrow doesn't strike true. The town and many of our businesses have sponsored group events, donated dates and exciting prizes for everyone to enjoy."

Mrs. Copeland frowned. "Now, for those of you who remember the little mishap from several years ago—" the frown tightened into a fierce glare that swept across the crowd "—never fear. Anyone nominated without their consent will have the opportunity to buy their way out of the events. But you must do it immediately because this get-out-of-jail option is only available tonight.

"But I'm certain we won't have anyone taking advantage of that this year. I've seen the list and I think our Cupid made some excellent choices."

Snapping open a piece of white paper with a huge

red Cupid watermarked right in the middle, Mrs. Copeland instructed the men to come to the stage to present small bouquets of pink-and-orange roses someone had prepared.

"Dennis Schroeder and Melissa Thompson." A boy—probably sixteen or seventeen--moved to the front of the room. A pretty blond girl jumped up and followed immediately behind him. She beamed up at him when he handed her the flowers and it was evident the two were already a couple.

The room buzzed with a myriad of emotions as name after name was read. Some people were obviously happy. Others were surprised. No one seemed upset...yet. Several of Lexi's friends were called away, although none of them appeared particularly excited about the prospect they'd been given.

Another name was read, one he didn't recognize. Gage didn't pay much attention, assuming the guy was an outsider, until Mrs. Copeland read out his sister's name. "Alexis Harper."

Beside him, his sister bounced out of her chair. With a wide smile on her face, he watched her wind through the tables up to the front of the room and realized he'd met the stranger, after all. It was the same guy who'd come in behind him at Sugar & Spice. And he did not like the way this guy was looking at his sister.

Gage clenched his hands beneath the table. His thumbs throbbed, but he ignored the pain. His entire body bunched with the intention of jumping up to wipe that satisfied smirk off his smug face. But a hand slapped down onto his thigh and tightened warningly.

"Don't," Hope breathed. "She knows what she's doing. She paid to be paired with him."

His eyes burned with the trapped heat of resentment when he turned them at Hope. But she didn't budge, and neither did her hand. In fact, her grip tightened. As if that was enough to keep him seated at the table if he didn't want to stay.

But somehow he found himself doing just that. He stared into her green-gold eyes and his hard muscles suddenly eased. The startlingly quick and disturbing need to lash out at something—the guy ogling his sister would have worked—disappeared.

He took a deep breath, filling his lungs with air that smelled just like her—crisp, sharp but somehow still mysteriously sexy.

"I've saved the best for last. Gage Harper."

Startled, he jerked away from Hope, grateful for the distraction. Until the reason Mrs. Copeland was calling his name sank in.

The entire room stared expectantly at him. After everything he'd been through in the past few weeks— torture, rescue, hospital, debriefing and media circus— being the center of attention should have been easy. It wasn't. Gage hated all the attention. How could having the barrel of a gun digging into the side of his skull feel less dangerous than having every eye in the crowd on him?

"I know most of you are aware of the events leading up to Gage's return home. And while we won't be getting into that this week, I'm certain no one will be surprised to learn that the committee recently voted to make the Wounded Warrior Project the beneficiary of this year's events."

Mrs. Copeland held out the final bouquet of roses and gestured toward him. Gage's gaze darted restlessly around the room, looking for anything or anyone that might rescue him from this moment. His eyes landed on his mother, the woman beaming at him. Next to her, his father sat tall and straight in the uncomfortable chair. For the first time he could remember, pride filled his eyes.

The shock of that reaction, more than anything else, had Gage standing. The entire room erupted into applause. Somehow he found himself beside Mrs. Copeland as she read out, "Hope Rawlings."

Murmurs bounced through the crowd, although he wasn't sure what they meant. Were they as shocked as he was? He wasn't sure how to react. Or what Hope might do. That's why he stood there, frozen, every muscle in his body tense.

She shifted restlessly on her chair and for a moment he was sure she was about to decline the match. Great. Of all the people they could have paired him with.

He wasn't even sure how he'd gotten on the damn list. Probably his mom. Or sister. He'd kill them later.

No doubt whoever this year's Cupid was had thought to do him a favor. Everyone knew he and Hope had been friends. Not everyone knew they weren't anymore. They'd probably figured Hope was safe.

Boy, were they wrong.

A frown rippled across Hope's face before she wiped it away. She obviously didn't want this any more than he did. Spreading his hips wide, he braced for what was coming as if he could find his center of gravity and counter the blow just like he had inside that ring.

To his surprise, it never came. Instead, Hope slowly pushed up from the table and began walking toward him. A hush fell over the crowd, the quietest he'd heard them all night. He wasn't the only one waiting to see what Hope would do.

The spotlight that had illuminated Mrs. Copeland swung to her. It bathed her in a golden light, making her warm blond hair glow.

Maybe she was just coming up front so she could look at the crowd when she announced that she'd be using that escape clause and paying to extricate herself from an unwanted week paired with him. But the closer she moved to the stage the less certain he was that she was going to reject the match. Her mouth stayed stubbornly shut, pressed tightly into a straight line.

Then it hit him. She couldn't do that without looking like a complete bitch. Thanks to his capture and rescue he'd become the town golden boy. No one would forgive her for rejecting him now—especially in front of a room full of strangers.

Gage opened his mouth to do it for her, but even as his lips parted, he realized the words wouldn't come.

Hope stopped in front of him. The room shrank down to just the two of them, everyone else fading away. He looked down into her bright eyes and realized they were full of dread and hope. Her hands stayed solidly at her side, clasped together, as if she didn't expect him to actually offer her the bouquet he was holding.

Her eyes pleaded with him. This was his chance for a little payback. To reject her publicly in front of the entire town.

He couldn't do it.

Slowly, he extended the flowers, offering them to her. The entire room sighed, as if they'd been collectively holding their breaths.

Gage was surprised to see a slight tremble in her

hand when she reached for the bouquet and brought it against her chest.

But Gage didn't relinquish the flowers. Instead, he let his knuckles brush against the soft satin of her dress and used the stiff stems to pull her into his body. Leaning down, he touched his lips to her ear and whispered so only she could hear.

"Watching you squirm is going to be so much fun."

5

WELL, SHE'D GOTTEN exactly what she wanted—Gage's undivided attention. Unfortunately, it took exactly thirty minutes to realize the plan was backfiring.

Hope desperately needed a few minutes away from the constant weight of his stare. Even from across the room, where she'd gone to grab a drink—finally—she could feel him watching her.

Jenna grasped her arm, yanked her out of line and dragged her through the swinging door into the small catering kitchen. "Oh, my Mary and Joseph, how did that happen?"

The moment the door shut behind them, blunting the music and laughter from the party, the rubber band of tension that stretched through her body eased. Her shoulders no longer felt tight enough to snap.

It should have been a relief. It wasn't. Instead, Hope found herself looking through the small round circle of glass cut into the center of the door, searching for someone she wasn't supposed to care anything about.

"Hope." Jenna shook her, pulling her attention back

where it should be. "Concentrate, girl. Why didn't you buy your way out of this? Gage Harper? Someone must be playing a joke."

"If they were I'd be the butt of it. How do you think it would have looked if I'd publicly humiliated the town hero? I couldn't have done that even if I'd wanted to."

Jenna opened her mouth before snapping it shut again. Her eyes narrowed as they searched Hope's face. Hope felt her skin warm beneath the too-keen stare.

"If you'd wanted to. Meaning you didn't want to."

She shrugged and glanced guiltily away.

"Hope Rawlings, what did you do?"

"Bought him," she mumbled beneath her breath. She hadn't meant to tell anyone, but somehow it made the guilt that had swamped her the moment Mrs. Copeland read her name a little easier to bear.

"You did what?" her friend screeched.

Hope slapped a hand across Jenna's big mouth. "Hush." They might be in the back kitchen, but that didn't mean the walls weren't thin enough for anyone on the other side to hear if Jenna was loud enough.

Jenna peeled Hope's fingers away and whispered around them, "Why the hell would you do that? Only a handful of people know about what happened, but… don't you think that's kinda cruel? The man told you he loved you."

"We were eighteen. He didn't know love from lust," Hope countered, although even she didn't quite believe that. But even if he had then—and she wasn't ready to admit that—he certainly didn't now.

"Is this because he almost died?"

"No," Hope protested, although the word didn't quite taste right. "That has nothing to do with this. I want that story, Jenna. If I can get it I'm pretty much guaranteed a job with the *Courier*."

Jenna stared at her. "This is about a *story?*"

"What else would it be about?"

Her friend frowned. "I don't know. Realizing you were wrong to let him go? Love? Isn't that what this entire week is about?"

"You thought…" Hope's words trailed off to nothing.

Jenna was happy to fill the void. "That Gage's brush with death forced you to admit you've always cared about him? Absolutely."

"Of course I care about him, Jenna."

Jenna made a rude sound in the back of her throat. "There's a difference between caring and *caring*. Not wanting to care and not caring aren't the same thing."

Hope stared at her friend, completely floored. This conversation was coming out of left field and she had no idea what to say.

Luckily the door to the kitchen swung open, saving her from having to come up with something. Unluckily, the person standing in the middle of the open doorway was Gage.

How long had he been there and just how much had he heard?

"There you are. I was worried you'd run away."

"Why would you think that?"

The line of his jaw flexed, but he didn't answer her. Instead, he crossed the small space, taking up more real estate than any one human had a right to. He crowded into her personal space. Why hadn't she worn her higher heels? At least then she'd have been able to look him straight in the eye.

Now she had to crane her head backward to peer up at him. It galled her, even that small yielding gesture.

"Everyone is waiting to see us dance together."

"Why? This isn't our wedding."

Gage chuckled deep in his throat. The sound drizzled down her spine like warm honey. "Not sure about your dad, but my mama is already addressing invitations in her head."

"That's her problem."

A sound of agreement rumbled through his chest. "Coward."

"Excuse me?"

"You heard me." He leaned forward until he was looking her straight in the eye, pinning her in place with that intensity again. "Hiding out in the kitchen."

Hope took a deep breath and said evenly, "I'm talking to my friend." Turning, she looked for Jenna, who was nowhere to be found. When had she disappeared? Where the heck had she gone?

"Uh-huh." The sharp edge of disbelief bled all over the sound. "That's what you've been doing back here for almost twenty minutes."

"I didn't realize I was being timed." Hope muttered.

"If you say so," he said. With a quick shrug of those massive shoulders and a deprecating lift to the corner of his lips, he slipped back out the door.

Oh, no, he did not. Hope's palm stung where she slapped it against the door.

Gage was twenty feet away when she shot back into the room. Several people turned to stare, but not him. Anger and resolve spurred her to grasp his arm and pull him to a stop.

"I'm no coward, Gage Harper, and never have been."

She went against him, toe-to-toe, rising up so she could get right in his face.

Heat and temptation roiled through his eyes, but that damn smile tugged at his mouth again. His arm snaked around her, a solid weight that bowed her back and pressed her body against his.

Out of nowhere he spun her. A small space opened around them, getting bigger as several couples cleared to the sides of the dance floor. Gage moved her effortlessly to the beat of the dramatic music pumping from the speakers around the room. Later tonight the mood of the party would change and current dance music would play, but for now the DJ was playing dreamy pieces that made her entire body throb with the possibilities.

Gage's thighs rubbed against hers. His fingers splayed low on her back, molding to her spine. Her cheek brushed against the curve of his shoulder. She could feel the dark heat seeping from him.

Her gaze strayed to the warm column of his throat. It was so close she could have reached out and run her tongue across the strong cord of muscle there. Would his skin be rough with stubble or smooth and just shaven?

What the hell was wrong with her?

He pulled her closer. "Why did you put your name in?" His breath stirred wayward strands of hair, tickling her cheeks and temple.

Awareness crackled across her skin. She tried to pull away from him, to put some space between them so that she could think, but he wouldn't let her. Like one of those Chinese finger traps, the more she struggled the tighter he held.

To Hope's relief, the eyes that had been watching them seemed to get bored and move on to more interesting action. "Why not? It's fun, it's for charity and I haven't had time for a date in months."

"Lexi said you haven't participated for several years."

"Did she also tell you that's because I was dating someone?" Maybe not seriously. Okay, she'd never dated anyone seriously. In college she didn't have the time. She'd had some scholarship money, but not enough to cover room and board. She'd worked off-campus, carried a full load and been on the school newspaper staff. As it was, graduating had taken her five years instead of four. Who had time for guys?

Then her father had gotten sick and she'd moved home. Taking care of him and keeping the paper running was all she'd had the energy to handle.

"No, she didn't mention that."

It was Hope's turn to let a satisfied smile curl her lips.

Unfortunately, it didn't stay there long.

Gage dropped his head into the curve of her neck. The warmth of his breath caressed her. Goose bumps cascaded down her shoulder.

The music stopped. So did they. Standing in the middle of the crowded floor, surrounded by people, she didn't notice a single one of them.

He stared down at her, his golden eyes glowing with blatant desire. She could feel the heat of him radiating through her. His skin, kissed from the desert sun, was a warm, rich brown.

If he'd looked at her like that twelve years ago would she have been able to resist him? Hope didn't think so. She'd fought her own fledgling, teenage craving for him, scared that if she gave in to it their friendship would be ruined.

He'd asked her out hundreds of times, but only as a joke. Or so she'd thought. And even if her hormones told her it was real, her head had always chastised her for indulging the fantasy. Gage had a new girl every weekend. He hadn't needed her. He didn't want her.

Then he'd told her he did, but in the next breath sent fear racing down her spine when he'd confided that he'd enlisted. Even if she'd been brave enough to risk their friendship, she couldn't risk caring about him only to lose him.

So she'd pushed him away. Severed all ties. And missed having her best friend in her life.

Hope swallowed, her throat so dry she couldn't have said anything even if her brain could come up with a coherent thought. Her entire body was on overload. Slowly, Gage extricated himself from their embrace and set her away.

Without a word he slipped into the crowd. She watched him go. If she wanted that story, she should stop him. But she didn't move after him. She couldn't, not if she hoped to keep her head and her focus. Maybe he was right, after all, and she really was a coward.

On shaky legs, Hope found her way back to the table and sank onto her chair.

"Well, hell, maybe I should have made a play for him."

Beside her, Tatum frowned into the dregs of the amaretto sour she'd sampled earlier.

"What?" Hope asked, trying to clear the buzz that dancing with Gage had left inside her brain.

Tatum gestured with the glass, a heavy drop of condensation dripping off the bottom and spreading unevenly across the deep red tablecloth. "Gage. You.

Steaming up the dance floor. If I'd known he was that combustible I might have broken some personal rules and made a play for him."

Hope stared at her friend. For about sixty seconds she contemplated offering Gage to her. She had at least six more days of this. How was she supposed to get through it without landing herself in serious trouble?

Gage was right when he said she'd been lying to herself about the past. She *had* been interested in him. Of course she'd wondered what it would be like if they were more than friends. If he hadn't been joking all the times he asked her out. What girl wouldn't have been drawn to Gage's good looks, commanding presence and that edge of danger?

But the moment he joined the army she'd been out. Losing her mother had devastated her. She'd been so young and so unequipped to deal with the sudden loss. Her dad had been there for her, but it wasn't the same. Not even he could fill the void. Gage had been there, as well, always knowing just what she'd needed to combat the ever present grief.

Which honestly made it all the worse. She couldn't do it. She couldn't love Gage and lose him. Maybe if he'd been different... But he wasn't. That streak of recklessness had scared the shit out of her. Gage was unpredictable. Brash and foolhardy. Daring and brave.

Now was no different. He was still the same man who embraced danger as if it were a long lost friend. Her resolve hardened. She had a week to get her story and she wasn't going to let anything stand in her way—especially not some long dormant physical reaction that she never wanted.

"MAN, SERIOUSLY, you have to come save me." Gage stared out the window of his childhood room at the full moon bright in the sky. The drink he'd barely touched was clutched in one fist; the other held his cell against his ear.

"It can't be that bad," Eli Weston countered. "You're a goddamn war hero. What the hell can they be doing to you?"

He sprawled back into the deep pocket of his mama's wingback chair. He'd probably catch hell for hauling the thing upstairs, but there wasn't a lick of furniture in the room big enough to fit him comfortably. He didn't remember being particularly scrawny as a kid, but the wooden chair tucked under the desk creaked ominously every time he tried to sit in it.

"You mean aside from smothering me, hounding me or staring at me with pity?"

"Let me call the sheriff," Eli drawled sarcastically. "That definitely qualifies as torture."

"Bite me."

"Naw."

This was exactly what Gage had needed, a conversation with someone who wouldn't tiptoe around him or flinch at accidentally using the word *torture* in conversation.

He needed a distraction. One that didn't smell good, feel amazing in his arms and go by the name Hope.

He, Eli and Micah had met in jump school. Even though they'd been assigned to different battalions, they'd remained close. They'd bonded, and nothing, not even Micah's death or his own screwup, could break that.

"The media is killing me. They're swarming all over town."

"You know if you'd just give them the interview they'd leave you alone."

"I can't do that." Guilt—both for what had happened and for not confiding in his friend—had him gulping down the finger of Scotch sloshing in the bottom of his glass. It was the only one he'd allow himself tonight. He'd seen too many guys try to drown the horrors of war with alcohol and it never ended well. He'd be damned if he'd take the easy way out.

"Your choice, man, but then you're gonna have to suck it up and deal."

Yeah, he knew Eli was right. He sighed heavily into the phone. That didn't make it any more of a picnic.

"Other than the reporters and crazy townspeople, everything else okay? You talking to someone about what happened?"

"Nah. I talked with someone at the hospital, but not since I left. I'm good, though."

"Don't be a hero—or an idiot. You went through hell. Find someone to talk to."

Gage gave a grunt that his friend could interpret as agreement if he wanted. But he had no intention of spilling his guts to anyone about what had happened. The people that needed to know had the details.

Gage's jaw tightened, his molars grinding together to combat the unwelcome images that flowed into his brain.

"Look, I didn't want to tell you this way, but I also don't want you to make the same mistake he did. Micah didn't die accidentally. He killed himself."

"What?" Gage jackknifed out of his chair. The last

dregs of his drink sloshed onto the floor. "What the hell are you talking about?"

"He killed himself. Took his gun and put a bullet in his own brain."

Gage knew Eli well enough to realize he was using the bluntness to cut through the fog of shock trying to wrap around him. Even as it attempted to take hold, Gage realized the information didn't surprise him. Not really. Hadn't he known that something about that night didn't fit? An accident cleaning his gun? Yeah, right.

So he'd asked for an assignment and against protocol followed a boy into a booby-trapped house, chasing after information. Intel that was just out of his reach. He'd been angry—with Micah, with the army, with the war and the world in general—and pushed harder than he should have, blinded to the signs that something wasn't right.

"I can't go through that again, man. So talk to someone. You were captured and tortured. No one can deal with that completely on their own. If you can't do it for yourself, do it for me."

Gage slowly sank back onto the edge of the chair. The shock was fading. Anger quickly replaced it. How could Micah do that?

"Dammit," he breathed. The edges of the cut crystal glass bit into his palm as his hand tightened. Without thinking his arm flashed forward. The glass crashed against the wall with a bang and a crunch. Shards rained down, hitting the carpet and disappearing. He wanted those breaking shards to sound as loud as the relentless ache in his chest. "Why would he do that? Why didn't he say something?"

"I don't know. I've been going over it in my head for

weeks trying to figure out if I missed the signs. I can't bury another friend, Gage. Not that way."

Guilt bit into him again. That's almost what Eli had been forced to do. Things could have turned out so much worse....

They were soldiers working in the middle of a war zone. Losing men was something they'd both dealt with and they all realized it was a part of the job. Dying in the line of duty was one thing. But suicide? It just felt pointless.

There were only so many promises he could make, but this was one he felt confident he could keep. "I promise that isn't going to happen. I'm okay. And if I start worrying that I'm not I'll find someone."

"And call me."

"And call you."

He and Eli talked for a little while longer. Gage told him about the Cupid charity event, although he didn't mention Hope. It was nice to hear his friend's laughter. It eased some of the tension that had been building inside him.

But soon after they hung up the silence of the darkened house pressed in on him again. His gaze was pulled back to the bits of glass that were sparkling at him from the floor. He should clean up the mess, but something wouldn't let him.

Those broken pieces were a reminder of his friend. A reminder of what he'd done and the role Micah's death had played in his own reckless decisions and the price other people had paid. Such a senseless waste— on all counts.

He needed to get out of there. It was Saturday night. Surely he could find another underground match.

Leaving the glass—he'd clean it up in the morning—Gage grabbed the keys to the Harley and headed out into the night.

6

Hope was exhausted. It was almost one in the morning. When had staying up past midnight become more of a chore than a treat? She was only twenty-nine. Wasn't she supposed to have endless energy?

Tigger, the orange tabby she'd rescued from a shelter in Charleston, met her at the back door. She didn't even have the energy to walk upstairs. Not yet. Instead, she leaned into the closed door and let her eyes slide shut as Tigger wound between her legs.

The feel of his soft fur was welcoming and reassuring. She'd moved out of her dad's house because it had been too difficult to stay. Nothing in that place ever changed. Her mom had chosen every stick of furniture and picture on the wall and her dad refused to get rid of any of it. He'd made the place into a shrine to the woman he'd loved and the life they'd lost. Everywhere Hope had looked there'd been a reminder of the mother she'd barely had a chance to know.

Those memories had only seemed sharper after almost losing her dad, too. Staying there felt wrong. It made her edgy, as if she was constantly waiting for more bad news.

But after moving out she'd been surprised to realize she was lonely. Tigger had been a friendly face to greet her no matter what kind of day she'd had.

Crouching down, she scooped him into her arms. He rubbed his head beneath her chin as she stroked down his soft back. He wasn't always this affectionate so she took advantage of it while he was cooperative. He must have really missed her.

Proving her right, about sixty seconds after she'd picked him up he started squirming to get down. She loosened her grip and he leaped through the air to land gracefully on the kitchen counter beside her.

With a sigh of relief Hope finally found the energy to flip her heels from her feet. As much as it grated on her ordered soul, she left them in a pile beside the door. She'd deal with them in the morning.

She didn't even bother to turn on the light, just headed across the open area that flowed from kitchen into living room. The floor plan of the house was perfect, and several times over the past four years she'd contemplated making an offer to buy the property. But she couldn't make herself do it. The couple she rented from were older and had moved into an assisted-living community. They'd probably have sold it to her if she asked, but she hadn't been willing to make that commitment. Buying property in Sweetheart…exactly the opposite of what she'd always wanted to do.

But she had to admit the space and quiet were nice. And why was she thinking about this now? Tonight? At one in the morning?

Frowning at her own wayward thoughts, she headed

for the stairs. Three bedrooms stretched invitingly into the darkness. One was a guest room that had rarely been used, the other was an office that saw more action than it probably should have. The third was her own oasis and held the promise of a bed she could fall into.

Before she'd even set foot on the first stair she reached behind and grasped the zipper of her dress. Efficient as always, she could multitask exhausted and in the dark. The tab was halfway down her back when a loud bang reverberated through the front of the house.

Tigger let out a protesting yowl and shot from the kitchen in an orange streak.

Hope pivoted on her heel and looked at the front door, wondering who could be knocking on it at this hour. No one used her front door, not even the pizza delivery guy, which made her pause. She couldn't actually remember the last time it had been opened....

A shadowy figure paced past the two narrow windows that ran on either side of the wooden panel. Male. Tall. Impatient.

Hope scowled and moved closer to see if she could identify the person audacious and rude enough to knock on her door at one in the morning.

"I know you're up, Hope. I just saw you drive in."

Gage. Hope slapped a hand across her stomach to try to stop the uncomfortable flip-flop thing it decided to do. The sensation was relief. Really. That was all. Relief at realizing the hulking figure wasn't a burglar trying to break into her house. Yeah, because burglars usually knock.

"Hope," he called again.

The man really was rude. She should ignore him. Let him pace out there as long as he liked. He'd disappeared from the party hours ago and then had the audacity to show up on her doorstep in the middle of the night?

But there was something in the agitated way he paced across her front porch. Or maybe it was the tone in his voice. Hopeful and desperate. Not once had she ever heard Gage Harper desperate. Not even that night when she told him they could never be together.

He'd always had a self-confidence that was intimidating and appealing all at the same time. Gage had always known what he wanted and didn't have a problem going after it; sometimes despite knowing he shouldn't. That kind of bravery...well, she reluctantly had to admit, probably made him an excellent soldier.

She had two choices. She could stand here and ignore him until he left. Or she could open the door and find out what he wanted. Everything inside her jangled a warning and told her to leave him out in the cold.

But her brain said letting him in was the logical choice. After all, if she had luck on her side—and maybe he'd had a few drinks since she last saw him— he might just spill his guts and save her an entire week of uncomfortable encounters. After all, she was supposed to be cracking him open like the spiny chestnuts that littered her dad's backyard.

With a sigh, she crossed to the door and jerked it open.

"What are you doing here?"

Gage stopped midpace and turned to look at her. His gaze started at the tip of her head and worked downward, although it got snagged right around the neckline of her dress.

Something dangerous flared deep in his eyes. Instinct kicked in and Hope stumbled backward, away from him and the unwanted wave of awareness that swamped her. Her hand found her throat again, wrapping around it protectively. With a gasp she realized thanks to her opened zipper the neckline was gaping and showing a heck of a lot more skin than she'd intended.

Spinning away, Hope reached for the zipper to jerk it back up, but her fingers were suddenly clumsy and the tab kept slipping through her grasp. Her shoulders strained as she contorted herself, trying to get the damn thing to cooperate.

Rough fingers brushed her hands away. A sure grip seized the tab. She could feel his hesitation, the pause as he decided whether to pull the zipper up or down.

Her breath caught in her lungs and held as she waited, too. Hope had no idea which she really wanted him to do. She knew what she *should* want, but apparently that didn't necessarily translate.

The sound of the teeth grinding together was louder than it ought to be. When the zipper reached the top of the dress Hope finally let the air leak from her lungs. Prematurely.

Gage ran a single finger across the top of her dress, letting it dip down beneath the line of fabric as he caressed her from one shoulder blade to the other. Hope jerked away, stumbling forward.

He stood there, his arms hanging innocently at his sides and his feet planted wide. He'd shut the door behind him, closing them both into the darkness of her home.

Having him there made her restless.

Hope's mouth twisted. "What are you doing here?"

she asked him again, hoping this time he might actually answer her.

"I have no idea."

That was not what she'd expected.

Hope shook her head. What was she supposed to do with that statement? Gesturing toward the living room, she told him to sit while she changed. If they were going to talk she definitely needed to get out of this dress. Not only was it starting to strangle her, but every time the zipper shifted against her spine her skin also tingled.

She debated about what to put on. What she really wanted was the soft pants and worn T-shirt she liked to sleep in. But somehow that felt too intimate, although Jenna would have argued that point with her. Hope could hear her voice right now, "Intimate is lace nighties and thin little straps that just beg a man to tear them off of you. Intimate is not paint-splattered and so big that you can walk on the hem of your pants."

Her friend might have had a point…if Hope had any intention of seducing Gage. Which she didn't.

Finally, she settled on a pair of stretchy leggings and a soft, roomy sweater that skimmed her thighs and was so threadbare she'd never wear it out in public. But it was so comfy. The kind of thing just made for a Saturday at home.

Technically it could still be considered Saturday since she hadn't been to bed yet.

Funny, the exhaustion she'd been fighting when she walked in the back door was nowhere to be found as she padded back down the staircase in bare feet.

She slid to a stop halfway down, shocked by the vision that waited for her.

Gage was sprawled in the corner of her favorite sofa.

The spot had the best light—soft in the morning, sunny in the afternoon. And when the moon was big and full, beautiful silver light illuminated it so brightly that she could read without needing a lamp.

Tonight the moon was dark, leaving him almost totally in shadow and making him look like a wounded angel. The bruises on his jaw only emphasized the impression. His head was dropped back against the overstuffed pillow. His eyes were closed, the inky circle of his lashes casting a shadow that made him appear even more vulnerable.

Vulnerable and Gage Harper—two things that did not go together. Ever. Even when he was putting himself out there, he had the ability to make you think that he was masterminding everything to work out exactly the way he wanted. She, better than most probably, knew that wasn't necessarily the case since he hadn't gotten what he'd wanted from her. But still, he'd always been so strong.

Tonight he looked broken, not that he didn't have every right to be. He'd been through a lot in the past several weeks. Hope's chest tightened uncomfortably as she watched him. Dread reared up unexpectedly and twisted through her. She should go upstairs and forget he'd even come by.

But she couldn't do that. Not tonight. Not when he looked like he really needed someone.

If his hand hadn't been moving rhythmically over Tigger's back she might have thought him asleep. Aside from that small, steady motion he was utterly still.

She could hear the motor of Tigger's purr all the way to the stairs. A spurt of jealousy surprised her.

Clenching her jaw against the illogical reaction,

Hope continued the rest of the way down. She stopped at the bottom of the stairs, her hand wrapped around the newel post, ready to bolt back up at the first sign that she needed an escape.

"He doesn't usually like people. Men especially."

Gage cracked his eyes open, looking at her from beneath weighted lids. "What makes you think he likes me?"

"He's sitting still. And purring."

His gaze dropped down to the cat. As if to prove her point, Tigger stretched his body up, following the path of Gage's hand to make sure he kept stroking.

"You missed him trying to take a chunk out of my hand. But we appear to have settled on an accord."

"So it would seem."

He lifted Tigger off of his lap and set him onto the floor. Her cat huffed, frowned up at the man who'd been petting him and stalked away with an indignant twitch of his tail.

Gage held his hand out, beckoning her to come sit beside him. With a shake of her head she rebuffed him. Instead, she curled her hands over the edge of her wingback chair.

The sooner she figured out what he wanted the sooner she could get him out of her home. Having him here made her…edgy.

Lines crinkled his forehead and his lips pulled down at the corners, as he unconsciously mimicked the glare he'd just received from Tigger. She wanted to reach out and smooth away the tension, to fix whatever had upset him. But that wasn't her job and Gage Harper wasn't her responsibility.

Thank God. She pitied the woman who fell in love

with the man sitting on her sofa, his thumbs bandaged from war, his jaw bruised from a fight he'd gone looking for and bone-deep sadness clouding his golden-brown eyes. He was the kind of frustrating, egotistical, mind-numbingly reckless man who sought out trouble just for fun.

Life was hard and painful enough without asking for torment.

In a few weeks Gage would leave again, returning to the kind of life where bullets and bombs were part of breakfast. And lunch. And dinner. The kind of existence where being captured, tortured and killed were constant possibilities. Her gaze fell to the hand he'd let drop back into his lap. The white bandage wrapped around his thumb made her heart ache.

Spinning away, Hope headed for the window. Maybe looking outside would be safe. Her eyes fell on the monstrously intimidating machine parked at the curb at the end of her front walk. Of course the damn man couldn't drive a nice, sensible sedan with side-curtain air bags and crumple zones. Nope, he had to lodge the equivalent of a rocket engine between his thighs and laugh at the wind and a need for speed.

Not that it was any of her business what he drove. The only thing she wanted from him was the story.

This was the perfect opportunity to press for her story. He'd come to *her* in the middle of the night. But she couldn't do it. The questions wouldn't come.

Maybe it was the way he'd looked when she'd come down, tired and...alone.

Hope heard the creak of her sofa, but didn't move. She felt the heat of him as he walked up behind her. His palms flattened against the glass on either side of her head. Her focus shifted from the Harley out her door to the reflection of the man who'd driven it.

She expected to find him watching her, but he wasn't. Instead, he was staring up into the endless night, a terrible expression on his face—grief and fury and guilt all raging inside him.

God, it hurt just looking at it. She couldn't imagine living with whatever was inside him.

Hope waited, her entire body tight with the desire to help him. But she had no idea how. What could she say when she didn't understand what was wrong?

Slowly, his gaze shifted downward until it snagged hers in the reflection.

"I...learned something disturbing about a friend tonight."

He stared at her, not saying more. And still, Hope waited. She couldn't tear her gaze from his. His breath panted in and out in short, shallow spurts. He let her see his internal battle, but that was as far as he let her in and it wasn't helpful because she didn't understand his turmoil. Was he trying not to say more or struggling to find the right words to tell her?

Their breaths mingled together, fogging the cooled glass and eventually obscuring his reflection. She needed to see him.

Twisting, Hope pressed her back against the window, putting as much space between them as his angled body would allow. It wasn't enough, but considering he had her trapped it would have to do.

"Tell me," she offered, quietly. It was the only thing she could do, let him know she was there and ready to listen, just like she'd always been when they were younger.

How many times had Gage come to her, upset over an argument with his father? How many times had she listened, giving him a sounding board and a place to vent?

Gage's eyes searched her face, sadness dulling their golden-brown depths. His lips parted and she thought he might kiss her. But then he closed them again and just shook his head.

Slowly, he bent his elbows. His body drew nearer. The heat of him increased, like the warmth of a fire.

He *was* going to kiss her. It was the logical expectation given the sequence of events. He'd only done it once before, their junior year during the Cupid festival. She'd been so surprised and overwhelmed. And then he'd laughed, like the whole thing was a joke. Her heart jerking inside her chest, she'd played along. Smacking his shoulder and acting outraged.

She wondered if he hadn't pretended that day, would things have been different. If he'd owned up to wanting her then, instead of waiting until he was leaving for a life filled with danger, could she have found the strength to tell him no?

Every cell in her body strained closer to him, wanting exactly what it shouldn't.

Kissing him back then had made her head fuzzy. She didn't like fuzzy. How much more potent would he be now?

Hope was desperately afraid she wouldn't survive the experience, at least not with her resolve intact.

Which is why she should have been grateful when his mouth overshot the target. Instead, he buried his head into the crook of her neck. His forehead rolled back and forth against her shoulder. His mouth, lips closed in a tight line and far from seductive, brushed against her skin. She felt the touch, anyway. The energy of it blasted straight through to her toes.

Her hands slid up, grasping his hips and holding on. His shirt bunched in her hands. A man this strong shouldn't be this exposed. Something about it was wrong. Hope wanted to hold on to him. To protect him—which was laughable since he was the toughest, most capable person she'd ever met—until whatever had made him vulnerable passed and he could pull back the edges of his hard outer shell.

They stayed there, wrapped together; the pane of glass pressed tight against her back as cold seeped through the bulky threads of her sweater. She didn't try to move.

"Thank you," he finally whispered, his voice hoarse and raspy.

"Fo—" Her own voice cracked. Clearing her throat, she tried again. "For what?"

Gage lifted away from her, pulling back until he could look straight into her eyes again. A single finger trailed softly across the curve of her cheek. "Letting me in."

The irony of that statement wasn't lost on her. She might have opened the door to him, but he was the one keeping her out. Keeping everyone out if she had to bet. Something had definitely upset him. And the fact that he'd come to *her* instead of his parents, his sister or any of the other friends he still kept in touch with, told her that he didn't really want to talk about it.

No doubt he'd come to her fully expecting to be rebuffed, so she'd been a safe choice.

She shrugged. What could she say?

His fingers tangled into her hair, tugging at the strands until she had no choice but to tip her head backward.

The kiss came out of nowhere. Maybe because she'd expected it earlier and let her guard down when it didn't happen. Because she hadn't been braced for it, the touch of his mouth overwhelmed her.

It should have been just as wild as he was. She waited for the danger and speed that he thrilled to, to spill out from him and flood her. Instead, it was sweet. Gentle. And probably more devastating.

Fierce and demanding she could have fought against. But the sweet coaxing and aching vulnerability that filled the warm question his mouth asked…how could she combat that?

He'd definitely improved from their first kiss, which meant she'd never stood a chance. Opening to him was the easiest—and most dangerous—thing she'd ever done. And the minute she did he swooped in and took much more than she'd meant to give.

His hands in her hair tightened, arching her neck and pulling her up onto tiptoe so he could get closer. His mouth ground against hers, finally giving her that biting taste of danger she'd expected. Too late.

Her own body betrayed her. Her hands grappled, getting tangled in his clothes as she searched for a better hold on him. One she'd never find.

Somehow her leg found its way to his hip, hooking around the jutting edge to press him tighter against her. If her hands couldn't do the job right…

Gage pulled away from her, breaking their kiss. A protesting sound rumbled through her chest. Where the heck had that come from?

They both panted, desperate to replace the oxygen they'd denied themselves. Just how long had they been locked together?

He stared at her with hot, serious, smoldering eyes. For a man who'd finally gotten a taste of what he'd always wanted, he did not look happy. Being kissed senseless and then frowned at had always been her secret fantasy, right?

He backed away, disentangling his hands from her hair. "I shouldn't have come."

She really wished she could agree with him on that. She wanted to. But she couldn't be upset that he'd come to her when he needed someone.

Without another word he left.

Hope stayed right where she was, sagging against the window. The rumble of the Harley rattled the pane of glass, echoing down her spine and jangling her already-sensitive nerve endings.

7

GAGE'S CHEEKS WERE FROZEN from cold and exposure. His fingers were stiff. He wasn't used to the South Carolina weather yet and had forgotten how cold it could get in the middle of the night.

He might have ridden until the sun came up if his aching thumbs hadn't forced him to give up. The weakness bothered him, but what could he do? They'd heal eventually or so the doctors had told him. Part of him wished they wouldn't, that they could stay a visible and painful reminder of the mistake he'd made so he wouldn't do it again.

The house was dark. His parents' car was in the garage so he knew they were home from the party. Although at 3:00 a.m. he would have expected them to be.

Letting himself into the house, he had an unpleasant flashback to his teenage years, sneaking in past curfew and hoping no one would notice. He shook the memory away. He was far from a teenager now.

Dropping the keys onto the counter, he didn't bother to turn on any lights as he moved through the house.

"You could have at least left a note." The hard voice startled him. Bright light flared on in the living room, momentarily blinding him.

He was losing his edge outside the danger zone, which was the only explanation for how his father had gotten the drop on him. If he'd been in Afghanistan it never would have happened.

At least he hoped.

"Excuse me?"

His dad unfolded his body from the sofa, slipping his hands into the pockets of his worn robe as he stood. It was the same dark gray robe the man had owned for as long as Gage could remember. That sense of déjà vu returned, right along with the urge to start spouting excuses for why he'd been out so late.

He bit back the words, clenching his jaw tight and grinding his molars together. He was not a kid, dammit, and hadn't been for a very long time. It was about time the old man realized that.

"Your mother worries, Gage. And after getting that visit in the middle of the night to tell us you'd been captured, I can't say that I blame her. Your friend Eli called your sister tonight, said you'd gotten some hard news and suggested we keep an eye on you. When your mother and I got home and you weren't here…"

He'd have a nice chat with Eli in the morning. Calling his sister. What did the guy think he was doing? But first things first. "Where's Mama?"

"Pacing in the bedroom."

"Dammit," he said without any real heat. Gage bent his head to stare at the ground and rubbed a hand over the back of his neck.

His dad took a step closer. "Don't blame your sister."

He jerked his gaze upward, but kept rubbing at the tightness invading his muscles. "I don't. Look, I don't know what you guys went through because I wasn't here, but I can imagine."

His father rocked back and forth on the balls of his feet. "I suppose you can."

"I needed to get out for a while. I took the Harley."

"So I noticed."

"That okay?"

"You know you don't have to ask."

No, he really didn't. Growing up he'd wanted nothing more than to take that bike out and open it wide so he could feel the wind slapping back against his face. His dad had never let him touch the thing.

With a sigh, he decided now wasn't the time to get into it. It was late and he needed to let his mama know that he wasn't a stain on a road somewhere.

But he couldn't stop himself from saying, "I'm not the same irresponsible eighteen-year-old boy I used to be."

"You don't have to tell me that, son. I was eighteen and indestructible once, too. It's hard when you figure out you're not. For me, that was the day you were born and I realized I was responsible for protecting another human being. Kinda changes things. Guess your epiphany was a little different."

Gage nodded. A lump formed in the back of his throat. He tried to swallow, but it wouldn't budge. So he ignored it.

"I'll go tell her I'm home."

His dad nodded, as well. "You do that," he said, and then sank back onto the sofa.

Gage saw the slight tremor in his hands before he clasped them tightly together in his lap.

And he wanted to break that damn glass against the wall all over again.

Or kiss Hope senseless so he could forget everything for just a few moments.

Because he couldn't do either of those things, he settled for knocking on his parents' bedroom door. "Mama?"

SHE HADN'T BEEN BOWLING IN…a very long time. It wasn't exactly high on her list of entertainment choices. But the bowling alley on the outskirts of town had closed to the public and donated all the lanes for the Cupid charity events. So she was standing with Lexi, Willow and Lanie waiting for her chance to get shoes.

And what paragons of fashion virtue they were.

Beside her, Willow sighed when the woman behind the counter handed her pair over. "Red, navy and black saddle shoes. What, exactly, are these supposed to go with?"

"Nothing," the woman offered with a smile. "They're ugly so no one will walk off with them."

"How's that working for you?"

"Not great. Apparently ugly bowling shoes are in."

Willow shuddered. "I beg to differ." As a highly sought-after couture wedding-gown designer, Willow would probably know.

"I'm guessing the teenagers swiping bowling shoes aren't interested in wedding white just yet," Hope offered.

Her friend cocked an eyebrow. "You'd be surprised. I

just got a call from an eighteen-year-old country music princess. She's marrying a high-profile race car driver."

"Beautiful. Maybe you can talk her into wearing these—" Hope held up her own excuse for footwear gingerly between thumb and forefinger "—as the perfect wedding accessory."

"I'd die first."

The woman behind the counter chuckled as they walked away.

Hope surreptitiously scanned the crowd of people milling around the twenty lanes. She wasn't sure which would be worse—Gage showing up or Gage standing her up.

He'd probably consider it payback to leave her hanging. Part of her wouldn't blame him. At least before last night.

That kiss changed everything, even if she didn't want it to. As tired as she'd been, she'd lain awake forever, tossing and turning, trying to suppress the buzz of energy that rippled through her whenever she thought of Gage's hands on her body.

She didn't want him.

No, that was a lie. She *shouldn't* want him. So why was she having trouble remembering that?

Possibly because the memory of that kiss was closely followed by the image of him on her sofa, broken and vulnerable like she'd never seen him before. But that should have made her resolve stronger, not weaker.

The man was a ticking time bomb, just waiting for the right moment to explode. She really didn't want to be in the vicinity when he did.

Unfortunately, she wasn't certain that was an option anymore.

If she didn't have the story…she might have been the one standing him up. Leaving the house, her feet had been leaden, trying to convince her to stay right where she was. But something stronger—and she wasn't entirely certain it had anything to do with dedication to her work—had her fighting her own instincts and moving forward.

Even now, though, she was contemplating the merits of leaving. The decision was made for her when Gage breezed through the door. He was so pretty. And dangerous. All cloudy eyes, darkly tanned skin and bulging muscles against straining black leather. He frowned, his sharp gaze sweeping purposely across the crowd. Until his eyes snagged on her and he jerked to a halt.

Heat blasted through her and her lips tingled. An expletive ricocheted through her, but somehow she managed not to let it out of her mouth. How was she supposed to concentrate when the sight of him sent her brain on a mental vacation?

The weather, always unpredictable in February, had turned on them. The collar on his jacket was flipped up against the biting wind that had blown in with the pregnant rain clouds. Behind him, droplets pattered against the glass door. Even from here she could tell his hair was damp, turning the coffee-colored strands almost black and making the ends curl against his neck. Had he gotten that wet walking to the door? Or had he ridden the Harley again…apparently without a helmet?

She'd bet money on the last one. Now that she thought about it, he hadn't had a helmet with him last night, either, had he?

Fury simmered deep in her belly. Stupid man. Why would he take that kind of unnecessary risk? What would have to happen to make him realize he wasn't bulletproof? Dying, that's what. Had he given the people who cared about him any thought—his parents, sister, her...everyone in town?

Apparently not.

Hope purposely turned away from him and plopped down into one of the connected chairs at the lane they'd been assigned to. With some fancy talking she'd managed to get Willow and her date assigned to the same lane as she and Gage. Lexi's group had already been full, but they did have the lane right beside them.

Lexi settled into the chair that backed up to Hope's and leaned close. "How are you doing?"

They'd spoken briefly last night at the cocktail party, but not much. The guy Lexi had been assigned to was an outsider, but if last night was any indication, she definitely seemed interested in him. And Hope had to admit the guy—Brandon was his name—appeared equally enamored with Lexi. But then, why wouldn't he be? The two of them had spent most of the night on the dance floor, seemingly absorbed in getting to know each other.

"Good. Fine." Her eyes strayed to Gage as he sidled up to the counter and grabbed his own hideous shoes.

Apparently the innocent gesture gave her away. "Uh-huh," Lexi hummed, doubt filling the sound.

Hope forced her eyes back to the knot she was tying in her laces. "Really. It's fine."

Gage stopped in front of them, grasped the ponytail Lexi had pulled her long blond hair into and tugged on it. "You and I need to have a friendly chat later, Piglet."

Guilt clouded Lexi's face, but she quickly cleared it away. "You know I hate it when you call me that."

"Then perhaps you should practice not squealing."

Lexi frowned. "There's a difference between squealing and protecting, Gage. I've only spoken to Eli a few times, but even I know he wouldn't make that phone call unnecessarily."

"You spoke to Eli before last night?"

Lexi shook her head. "How do you think he had my number? When you were…" Lexi's words trailed off and her eyes dulled.

Hope reached out and placed a supportive hand on her shoulder. Lexi gave her a small, weak smile.

"Gone," she finally said. "We talked several times. He was very helpful and hopeful. A good friend."

The tight line of Gage's jaw flexed, but he gave her a single curt nod, acknowledging that she had a point. "He is."

Hope didn't quite understand what was going on, but she wondered if it had anything to do with his late-night visit to her house. The middle of a crowded bowling alley was not the place to ask, though.

Apparently feeling her point had been made, Lexi jerked her chin up and turned her back on them. Gage sank heavily into the chair beside hers. His shoulders curved in on themselves for the space of a few breaths before he purposely straightened them.

The chair obviously wasn't big enough. The hard seats were connected together, nothing more than a row of indented plastic bowls, which meant there was nothing she could do to put space between them. From his left, his wide shoulder and heavy thigh brushed against her. It was either let him rub up against her as he bent down to tie his shoes, or crowd as far into the opposite side of her scooped seat as she could.

She went with that.

She and Gage, along with Willow and her date, Max—an accountant who worked with the only firm in town—were assigned to one lane. The one connected to them had two teenagers who were obviously dating—they couldn't keep their hands off each other—and another couple she'd never met. They were in their early twenties so she wasn't surprised that they hadn't crossed paths before. And if the awkward way they were tiptoeing around one another was any indication, they were seriously interested in each other.

A voice crackled over the intercom, "Everyone ready?" Suddenly most of the overhead lights dimmed, plunging the bowling alley into gloomy shadows. Another set of lights popped on in their place—black lights—making the swirling designs painted on the walls glow.

At the end of the lane the pin mechanism whirred. When it lifted Hope realized the pins were glowing, too. Moody music pumped through the speakers, thumping deep in her chest.

Gage grinned down at her, his teeth gleaming. Shrugging his shoulders, he shed the black jacket, revealing a plain white T-shirt that radiated light.

"This is going to be fun." His voice was dark, and throbbed with a promise that her body determined had nothing to do with knocking down pins. Suddenly the middle of a Sunday afternoon felt more like midnight.

"I haven't bowled in years."

Standing up, Gage rolled his shoulders and neck, cracking it even as he reached for one of the balls waiting in the rack. Without hesitation, he stepped up to the line, settled the ball in his hands, walked a few steps and then let it fly. The rhythmic motion of his body was so

smooth and mesmerizing that Hope wasn't even paying attention to the ball rolling down the lane until he
let out a whoop of victory and the clatter of falling pins
registered in her ears.

Every last one of them rolled haphazardly across
the floor.

"Is there anything you're not good at?" she blurted
out without thinking.

Gage stopped midstride on his way back to the seat-
ing pit. Loud enough for everyone to hear five lanes
over, he said, "Getting you to say yes."

Behind her, Lexi snickered. Willow smothered a
laugh with her hand. Hope felt heat race up her face.
Thank God it was dark and no one would notice.

Gage dropped down beside her, his eyes locked onto
her face. No one but Gage.

"Didn't that hurt your thumb?" she croaked out, trying to fill the space between them with something.

"Yes."

That was it. No explanation. No excuse. Just a calm,
immediate acceptance of the pain. For a game.

"Then why are you bowling?"

"Because I can." The rough pad of a single finger
ran softly down the length of her cheekbone. "Because
you're here."

Hope jumped up, nearly knocking poor Max out of
his chair. To cover her reaction, she grabbed for a ball
and walked to the line.

She had no idea what she was doing. Maybe if she
hadn't been flustered, what little she remembered from
her infrequent childhood visits to the bowling alley
might have resurfaced, but the minute Gage touched
her her brain had checked out.

Mimicking Gage's movements, she settled the ball in front of her, took several steps and sent the heavy weight careening down the lane. Twenty feet down the ball rolled drunkenly into the gutter, nowhere close to hitting a single pin.

With a sigh of dissatisfaction, Hope spun around, not wanting to watch the ball finish its pathetic roll. But as she reached the drop-off back into the pit Gage was there waiting. He blocked the path and wouldn't let her down.

"You've got another turn."

"What if I don't want it?"

Gage stood below her, just enough that their eyes were perfectly level. His gaze bored into hers, demanding something from her that she didn't want to give. "Since when are you a quitter? As long as I've known you, when you want something nothing can stand in your way. Including me."

That was completely different. He was comparing her entire life plan to a silly game. "This game hardly matters, Gage."

"Maybe not, but you're still letting it beat you."

With a grumble of exasperation, she grabbed for the ball as it popped back into the return. "Happy?" Spinning around, she cradled it in her arms and prepared to chuck it down the lane as fast as possible, but she didn't make it.

He plucked it out of her grasp, leaving her hands frustratingly empty. Did the blasted man want her to bowl or not?

"First—" he set the ball back into the return "—that ball is too heavy for you."

"It's the same one you used."

"Precisely."

"Are you calling me weak?"

"No, I'm calling you a woman." His eyes raked her from head to toe, backing up the statement and sending a prickle of awareness seesawing through her. "Your body is built differently and you can't throw as much weight as I can. Fact, not judgment."

Her first urge was to say *watch me*. Logic kept her from spouting off and saying something she'd regret. He was right, even if she didn't want him to be.

"All right. Which one should I use?" she asked, waving her hand across the group of waiting balls.

He spun all of them, quickly rejecting four before he finally settled on the fifth. Grabbing the green ball with marbled blue veins, he dropped it into her waiting arms. She had to admit it was a heck of a lot lighter.

Grasping her shoulders, he spun her around and marched her back to the dotted line on the floor. He wrapped his arms around her, the solid length of him pressed tight against her back. Her skin tingled where they touched. He kept talking to her, as if she could actually pay attention to anything he was saying with her brain short-circuiting.

His large hands cradled her own, positioning her grip on the ball.

"We're going to take three steps forward. Thrust the ball out, let it swing back and on the third step, when it moves even with the lane, let it go."

"You make it sound easy." And possibly dirty.

"It is."

His knees bent, nudging the back of her thighs and sending her forward in the first step of the dance. Suddenly, the ball was whooshing past her hip. "Bend your knee," he ordered straight into her ear. Her body did exactly as he said, dropping down into a crouch as she released the ball.

It fell onto the surface of the lane with a heavy clunk, but instead of swerving immediately to the side, it stayed in the center, heading straight for the pins at the end.

It was her turn to let out a surprised whoop when it actually connected and several pins rattled onto their sides.

She spun around to grin at Gage. He stared at her, a strange expression on his face. Slowly, her smile faded and her chest tightened.

8

HE WANTED HER.

So what was new? He couldn't remember a time when he hadn't wanted Hope Rawlings. She was strong, determined, beautiful, caring. What man wouldn't want her? When everyone else in his life had thought of him as a screwup, Hope had always been there telling him he was worth more.

But this was different.

He was different.

No longer a green boy with nothing to offer her but the chip lodged firmly on his shoulder. The problem was he didn't think that would matter. If she hadn't wanted him back then, when they'd been closer than he'd ever let any woman get, then why would she want him now?

Especially since he was exactly what everyone had always accused him of being. What she'd accused him of being last night—blinded by a reckless need for danger.

Willow walked past them, breaking the spell. "Quit hogging the lane, you two. It's my turn."

Galvanized by her friend's statement, Hope dropped her gaze and slipped past, being careful not to actually touch him.

Yeah, that wasn't going to work for him.

For the next hour they bowled. And every chance he got he brushed against her. He purposely let his knees fall open so they'd touch hers. Whenever she stood to pick up her ball he let his fingers slide across her hip.

His plan was to set her off-kilter. However, he made a serious tactical error in not factoring his own physical response into the battle plan. By the middle of their second game his entire body buzzed with tension and need.

It was damn difficult to bowl with a perpetual hard-on.

Somewhere along the way Hope stopped looking him directly in the eye. Part of him had to think that was a good sign, that she didn't trust herself to without doing something she'd regret.

Which is exactly what he wanted to push her to do—although he had every intention of making sure neither of them regretted anything.

Throwing him a mumbled excuse, Hope walked away. He expected her to head for the snack bar or the ladies' room. When she beelined for the front door the only thought he had was *hell, no.* She was not going to run away and leave him here alone.

Gage shot to his feet. He was halfway across the space before he realized she'd left her purse sitting beneath her seat. She couldn't be trying to duck out on him.

So what was she doing outside in the rain?

Even beneath the long overhang covering the front of the building, a fine mist filled the air. Beyond that a steady sheet of rain turned the late afternoon into a drab gray wall.

At the far end of the overhang, Hope leaned against the metal building and stared out into the rain.

He knew the moment she noticed him, as she jerked away from the wall and stood straight.

"I needed some air. It's stuffy in there."

The flush across her skin suggested she was telling the truth. He had to think the eighty odd people inside had something to do with it. Because he was feeling the same way—severely claustrophobic. Penned in by everyone else when what he wanted was to be alone with her.

She stared warily up at him. He took a step closer. Her feet shuffled and she moved backward, straight into the steady drip of rain from the lip of the roof above them.

Air whistled through her teeth as she sucked in a gasp. The shoulders of her shirt were soaked even though she was only there for a heartbeat. Crystalline droplets glistened in the crown of her hair. She shook her head, dislodging them. Several hit him square in the chest, leaving perfect circles of moisture.

With an expletive, she reached up and ran her hands through her damp hair, pushing off any remaining water.

She was beautiful and they were alone, cut off from everything and everyone by the walls and rain.

Surging forward, Gage grabbed her and crushed her against him. He devoured her, taking everything that he'd ever wanted from her. She didn't stop him. That was all the invitation he needed to keep going.

Her back bounced against the wall, the sound of rippling metal crashing right along with the thunder of the storm. Water washed down his back. He wasn't sure where it came from. Had his momentum pushed them both out in the middle of the downpour? Did it matter?

Her arms wrapped around his neck, boosting her up so that she could get a better angle on their kiss. She practically climbed his body, anchoring her legs around his waist so that she could tower above him. And he was perfectly happy to have her there. Have her anywhere.

He tugged greedily at the hem of her shirt, yanking it from the waistband of her jeans until he could find bare skin. She gasped, breaking their kiss when his fingers grazed the plane of her belly.

Her eyes smoldered at him from beneath lowered lids. Water droplets collected in the hollow of her throat. Dipping down, he licked them away, loving the rain-soaked taste of her skin.

She shuddered and dropped her head backward to give him better access.

"Hope, where are—"

Together, their heads swiveled to look at the half-opened door and Willow standing there, staring at them, her mouth open wide enough that if she'd move two feet forward she could drown.

Her jaw snapped shut. She cleared her throat. "Yeah, it's your turn, but I'm guessing you're not coming back to the game."

"What makes you say that?" Hope asked, her voice soft and steady, as if she didn't currently have her legs wrapped around Gage's waist and his hand wedged between them both.

Willow's eyes widened. He could have sworn that wasn't physically possible a few seconds ago.

"Well…" She waved a hand at them as if she didn't need words. She found some, anyway. "You're a little wet."

Gage turned to look at Hope. She looked like a drowned cat. A very adorable one, but still…

A loud burst of laughter shot through him. He shook with it. Tears of mirth clouded his vision. He worried about dropping Hope so he tightened his arms around her and scooted them several feet farther beneath the awning.

She stared at him, mutely, her expression a combination of surprise, concern and a tinge of "he's gone crazy."

Her dark blond hair hung in heavy chunks over her shoulders. Water dripped down her body from the wet strands. Her clothes were completely soaked and suction-cupped to her body tight enough that anyone looking would be able to tell what cut of panties she preferred.

That did not sit well with him.

"Could you do us a favor and bring Hope's purse?" he finally asked Willow.

"Uh-huh," she answered. A few minutes later she rematerialized with it and their shoes tucked under her arm. "I had to do some fancy lip work before they'd give me your shoes, so don't make me a liar."

She waited, her arms crossed over her chest, while they both changed. Hope's socks squelched when she stuffed them into her runners. She grimaced. "These'll never be the same."

"I'll buy you new ones," he promised.

"No, you won't."

Willow disappeared back inside, leaving them to their argument.

"Why not? I'm the one who pushed you out into the rain."

"Did you see me protesting?" she asked.

No, no, he hadn't.

"I'm perfectly capable of taking care of myself, Gage. I don't need you to do anything, including buying me shoes."

Something about the way she said that bothered him, but considering he currently had a beautifully outlined view of her entire body, his brain was otherwise occupied and didn't have anything left over to puzzle out why.

The thought of picking up where they'd been interrupted was tempting, but there was no guarantee it wouldn't happen again. And the next time he got his hands on her, he wasn't stopping—for anything or anyone. And while the idea of taking her against the side of the building in broad daylight didn't bother him in the least, he didn't think Hope would appreciate being naked for the entire world to see.

Goose bumps popped up on Hope's arms. Besides, it was too cold to stay out here in wet clothes. She might catch pneumonia and then where would he be?

"Stay here," he ordered. To make sure she wouldn't slip away, he grabbed the purse Willow had set against the wall before darting out into the rain.

"Hey!" she yelled after him. "What do you think you're doing?"

"Taking you home," he shouted back.

"I can drive myself," she muttered beneath her

breath. He'd parked the bike close enough that he could hear her.

Opening the saddlebag, he pulled out the spare helmet his dad stored there and replaced it with her purse. Settling onto the seat, he cranked the engine, ignoring the way his rain-soaked jeans strangled his thighs.

Gage pulled straight onto the walk beneath the roof. Hope jumped backward, plastering herself against the metal wall.

"What the hell do you think you're doing?"

Hadn't he already answered that? "Taking you home," he said again, a little slower so that maybe she'd get it this time.

"I'm not going anywhere on that thing. Especially in the rain. With you, Mr. Speed Limits Are Merely A Suggestion."

"You're already wet, Hope. Do you really want to ruin the interior of your car? The sooner you get on, the sooner you'll be in dry clothes."

She wrinkled her nose. He held the helmet out to her.

As she crossed her arms over her chest, all the blood in Gage's body temporarily relocated to his groin. The glare she gave him was no match for wet clothes and the high, firm breasts pushed against soaked clothing.

"Where's your helmet?"

"Don't need one."

"It's the law."

Gage laughed. That was twice in the space of a few minutes. The bubbling, effervescent sensation felt rusty, but really good.

"Do you really think Sheriff Grant is going to cite me for that? I don't think so. I'm the town hero, Hope. I can do whatever I want."

"That doesn't mean you should. Gage, you need to wear a helmet. Don't make me write one of those stories."

"What stories."

"You know, the ones where the soldier lived through harrowing moments of war—like being captured, tortured and rescued—only to be killed at home because the idiot refused to wear a helmet while riding his Harley."

Something dark curled through his chest. No, he didn't want to be remembered that way. But there was something…seductive about the idea of going out with a fiery bang. Everyone died. The idea of slipping away quietly in his sleep had never appealed to him. He wanted to die with adrenaline pumping through his veins and a rebel yell echoing through his lungs.

He wanted to greet death with bared teeth and a dare.

He just didn't want to do it today. Or next week. Or thirty years from now. And certainly not before he'd touched, tasted and explored every inch of Hope Rawlings's breathtaking body.

Now that was an exhilaration he desperately wanted to experience.

And while he had no problems taking risks with himself, he'd be damned if he'd let Hope. The vision of her broken beneath the wreckage of his dad's bike left him feeling queasy and desperately uneasy. "I only have one helmet with me right now."

"Then I'll drive my car home."

"Wouldn't matter. This one's too small for me."

He waited. They were at a standoff, neither one of them willing to budge. Slowly, she said, "Promise me you'll wear a helmet from now on."

It was easy to say, "All right," even if he had no intention of actually following through with it. Whatever he needed to say to get her on the back of the bike, he'd do. Because he was afraid if he let her out of his sight somewhere between here and her house, the girl who'd spent their childhood challenging him, telling him no and looking at him crossways when every other girl had panted after him would resurface.

Reluctantly, Hope took the helmet and shoved it down over her head, clipping the tiny straps beneath her chin.

With a sigh, she flung her leg over the side and wrapped her arms around his waist as if he were the only thing between her and certain death.

Which was just fine with him.

When he was sure she was settled Gage shot out into the rain. He whipped his head back, laughing up at the sky, daring the storm to do its worst.

He hadn't felt this great in…ever.

GAGE PULLED TO THE CURB in front of her house. The bike purred between her thighs for several seconds before he turned it off. She wished it were that easy to switch off the energy thrumming inside her. Unfortunately, it had nothing to do with the bike and everything to do with the powerful man controlling it.

Swinging her leg off, she pulled the helmet from her head and dropped it onto the seat. Somewhere along the twenty-minute ride the rain had petered out to an annoying drizzle. Fumbling inside the saddlebag, she fished out her purse and darted for the back door.

He followed her, but then she'd expected him to. As much as she might like to pretend the episode at the bowling alley hadn't happened…it had. And they needed to deal with it.

Bursting inside, she dropped her purse onto the counter and whipped her hands forward to shake off the water droplets covering her arms. Water puddled on the floor. Tigger darted out from the den, took one look at the water and disappeared again.

Hope bent, pulling at the laces of her waterlogged shoes. "I'm going to—" she began from her folded position as she struggled with a reluctant knot, but the rest of her words died in her throat.

Gage wrapped his arms around her from behind and pulled her into his body. He spun her around and pressed her against the kitchen counter. Off-kilter, she had one shoe off and one shoe on. Three seconds ago all she'd wanted was to get into dry clothes. But considering the sharp heat singeing her, now all she wanted was to get out of her clothes—wet, dry, who cared?

His mouth claimed hers. She'd expected hot and hard, instead she got soft and coaxing. The first she'd been braced for. The second was more devastating because it was so stunning.

Her slippery fingers spread wide across the granite countertop, searching for something solid. His hand swept roughly up her nape, angling her neck and pulling her closer. Her knees buckled. How could that happen? She didn't want that to happen. Didn't want him to have the ability to send her to her knees, literally.

Not that she had a chance to really examine the situation. Not with his hands tearing at her shirt. He pulled the wet material over her head. It squelched when it dropped to the floor. She couldn't stop the grimace and brief urge to rush over and clean up the mess that it was undoubtedly making of her floor.

But he distracted her by pulling his own shirt off with one quick motion. This time she barely heard the liquid *splat*.

Hot muscle against cool skin. There was nothing else but him pressed against her. She couldn't breathe. Couldn't think. Couldn't want anything but him.

His feverish lips latched onto her throat. "Tell me to stop," he groaned roughly. "But say it now because in a few minutes I won't be able to let you go."

Like he was playing fair. "Why don't you stop kissing me and say that again."

He laughed against her, the sound vibrating through her. Her skin felt paper-thin, not strong enough to hold him out, or her in.

"Haven't you heard? All's fair in war."

Love and war. But she wasn't about to correct him. Not now.

And still, he took a single step back. His hands dropped from her body to ball into fists at his side. His biceps bulged, long lines of bluish veins popping out in provoking relief. His pecs and abs hardened, straining against the same need that coursed through her own body.

"Tell me to leave, but do it now."

Delicious desperation filled his voice. Never in her life had she been this overwhelmed by a man.

Or this desired.

How had she ever found the strength to tell him no? That she couldn't care about him?

Holding her hands out, she motioned for him to come back to her. It was all the answer he needed.

The catch of her bra snapped and fell away. His hands dropped to the fly of her jeans, but there they hit a snag. Desperation—his *and* hers—fought against rain-soaked denim. Her jeans clung to her skin, reluctant to release the hold they had on her thighs.

Gage had her pants bunched into an unyielding ball halfway down the curve of her rear. With a growl, he picked her up and plopped her down onto the counter. The cold granite might have been a shock to her system if she hadn't already been chilled from the rain.

With the change of leverage, he wrapped both hands into the waistband of her jeans and yanked the suckers away. They, too, landed with a squelching plop.

"Good place for them," he said, pointing accusingly at the jeans, as if they might become ambulatory and try to prevent him from having her again.

She moved to jump down off the counter, but his heavy hold on her thighs stopped her. His hands were so big. Strong. Capable. He could do anything with those hands, anything he wanted. Spread wide, they could have wrapped all the way around her leg.

His fingers, agile, calloused and marred by a myriad of tiny scars, held on tight. The bandages on his thumbs made her chest tighten and ache. She stared at them, mesmerized and momentarily overwhelmed by everything—him, her, them.

"Don't," he growled, low and threatening.

She jerked her gaze up to his. "Don't what?"

"Don't think about it. Don't let them win. Don't ruin this."

Her throat tightened, but she nodded. How could she not? It was the only thing that she could do for him. She hadn't been there. She couldn't protect him. Couldn't prevent the suffering. So she'd give him this instead, even if it hurt her just a little to do it.

Reaching for him, she spread her thighs wide and pulled him into the waiting cradle. Even as his hands moved tantalizingly up the inside of her thighs she struggled against a need to hold on to him.

A need to feel him and know that he was there. Safe.

To hide the reaction—from him and herself—Hope pulled his mouth to hers and let the desire she'd been struggling against fill her. It was so much easier to deal with than the rest.

His tongue stroked against hers, tantalizingly insistent. An arm swept her hips forward, balancing her precariously on the edge and bringing her aching core tighter against him. Wet denim abraded her warm thighs.

Her hips rolled against him. The reaction was involuntary, instinct and need. She ached to feel him, all of him, deep inside her.

A sound erupted from his throat, a combination of wounded surrender and snarling command. She understood perfectly.

It was so liberating to stop fighting against them both. Such a relief.

His mouth and hands were everywhere. Her throat, shoulders, stomach. His teeth grazed against the distended tip of her breast. It was her turn to whimper. She watched that damnable smile play with the edge of his lips as he opened them. She could feel the moist heat of his breath on her aching flesh, and still he wouldn't give her what she wanted.

His golden eyes glittered.

"Gage," she warned.

"Hmm," he answered, the sound buzzing deep in the back of his throat.

As she watched his tongue flicked out for a single, quick taste of her. How could that one touch send a shudder convulsing through her entire body?

Her eyes slid closed at the pure pleasure as he did it again. But he didn't let her luxuriate long.

"Look at me." Her eyes popped open, obeying without question. "I want you to watch what I do to you. I want you to see. To know it's me."

How could she not? Only Gage had ever made her feel this restless and out of control. That's what had always scared her. When they were fourteen, fifteen, seventeen, just the weight of his eyes on her could make her skin feel tight enough to split and spill out everything she was. All she could think of back then was if he could make her feel that way without even touching her...

That kind of power and control still scared her. But it was a little late for second thoughts. Besides, the pleasure of him was a heck of a lot stronger than the fear.

His mouth trailed down her body. "I've waited years for this. I'm going to relish every second. I'm going to draw it out and make it so good that neither of us will ever be able to forget."

That sounded...decadent and terrifying and absolutely perfect.

"Like I could."

Muscles leaped everywhere his lips touched—her belly, her hip, the crease at the top of her thigh. His tongue swept beneath the edge of her panties, making her gasp.

His mouth latched onto her through the barrier of lace and satin. Her hips surged forward—she wanted so much more. The heat of his breath caressed her. It wasn't enough.

One large hand lifted her up as the other yanked away the final barrier between them. He stared at her bared body, studying her with an intensity that had her squirming self-consciously.

She was far from a virgin, although her first real sexual encounter hadn't been until college. At home she'd never been interested in anyone. Spending all her time with Gage, she'd had nothing left over for anyone else.

Besides, she'd never thought of herself as a particularly sexual person. She liked sex. Who didn't? It felt good. But nothing—not a damn thing—could have prepared her for the way Gage made her feel.

Every cell in her body was awake, straining to get closer to him. To get more of him. It was an energy writhing inside her. A need so inherent and deep she was afraid she'd never be able to shake it.

And maybe that's really why she'd kept him at a distance.

Gage dropped to his knees in front of her. She wanted to protest, but couldn't find the words.

A stubble-roughened cheek rubbed back and forth against her inner thigh. Her skin prickled and tingled.

"It isn't fair," he whispered against her.

His hands spanned her hips. A single thumb brushed softly against the curls he'd just uncovered.

She ached. So badly. "What isn't?"

He spread her open. Cool air kissed her heated skin, driving her crazy.

"That you can be this beautiful."

Hope scoffed, the harsh sound crackling and breaking. "I'm not." Willow was classically beautiful. Lexi was cute. Tatum was edgy and mysterious. Macey was soft and comfortable. Lanie was striking. Jenna was confident. She was pretty…and realistic.

He looked up at her, staring her straight in the eye. "You are." When he said it that way, all heavy words and honest gravity, she almost believed it. "I've met women from all over the world—exotic, appealing, even seductive."

"Just what every girl wants to hear when she's naked and vulnerable."

"The only one who's vulnerable here is me. I've wanted you for as long as I can remember, Hope. and you know that. *You* have been the woman I compared every other to."

Hope tried to laugh off what he'd just said, but the sound got strangled. "Only because I told you no. If I'd said yes, if I'd followed you to basic training and hung around like some army groupie, you would have been bored within a week."

"Not true. Plenty of women have told me no over the years. I just didn't care when they did. With you, that 'no' hurt."

What was she supposed to do with that? As she sat naked on her kitchen counter, his words made her feel even more exposed, which was silly since he was the one making confessions.

She didn't want to be the standard he used for other women. She didn't want to have that kind of responsibility and power in his life.

She didn't.

Hope leaned forward and tried to push him away from her. Tried to close her thighs and block him out.

But he wouldn't let her.

"Oh, no, you don't. You don't get to run away this time, Hope. I'm not letting you."

His mouth latched onto her sex. The silky edge of his tongue stroked her clit. And any thought of protecting herself, of denying him, fled.

It was too late, she'd already let him in.

His fingers slipped up the slit of her sex, spreading the evidence of her desire for him. Her heart pounded erratically in her ears and everything but the feel of him faded away to nothing.

He stroked her, teased her, drove her to the brink of insanity. And she relished every second of it.

Gage pulled her tighter against his tormenting mouth, balancing her on the edge of reality and the counter. Her hands scrabbled for something solid to hold on to even as the storm of sensation built dangerously inside her.

Her entire body strained. She'd never been this overwhelmed or wantonly desperate.

A cabinet door crashed open. Several thunks reverberated ominously. Tigger yowled from wherever he'd hidden. Her fingers curled around whatever she'd grabbed on to, the sharp edge of something biting in and holding on.

Her hips thrust against Gage's relentless mouth. His tongue speared deep inside her. And she broke apart into tiny pieces. Her entire body bucked against the snap of release. Hot pleasure washed through her, blinding her to everything but the way he made her feel.

She screamed. Or maybe that was just in her own head. She didn't know. Didn't care.

Finally the world stopped spinning and everything settled back into place. Hope opened her eyes—it was the first indication they'd closed. Gage was standing before her, staring down at her with a hot, dangerously self-satisfied grin. The remnants of her passion glistened on his lips. She should probably be embarrassed by her own abandon, but she wasn't.

How could she when Gage was finally smiling? Really smiling. Not that weak excuse for the joy and excitement he'd always found in life, but the genuine thing.

She'd done that. Well, she supposed he'd done that. But she was about to make that smile of satisfaction even wider.

Something skittered across the granite countertop when she shifted. For the first time she looked around her and nearly choked on laughter.

Several small bottles lay scattered around her. Her spices. The cabinet door next to her swung drunkenly back and forth.

Looking back at Gage, she wrapped her hand in the waistband of his jeans and pulled him closer. "One of us is going to have to clean up this mess and it isn't going to be me."

"Happy to. Rearranging your spice rack is a small price to pay for having you."

"Is that what they're calling it these days?" she whispered against his mouth.

Heat and need slammed through her. How could she want him again so quickly? "Take me upstairs."

She didn't have to ask twice. Gage swept her off the counter and into his arms, heading straight for the staircase.

9

WET DENIM CONSTRICTED painfully against his straining cock. Taking them two at a time, Gage bounded
up the stairs. If he didn't find a bed in the next thirty
seconds he was going to take her right in the middle
of the hallway.

And while that might have been one of the fantasies
his teenage mind had played out all those years ago, he
thought he'd gained some control since then. Apparently
not. Not where Hope was concerned.

At the top of the stairs four doors lined the hallway.
Bedrooms? Bathrooms? An office? She saved him by
saying, "Last door on the right."

He strode across her bedroom, a red haze of need
clouding everything but his focus on her.

Her hair was damp against his arm. His own skin felt
clammy and tight, as if the rain had pounded straight
into his pores. He wanted a shower, but he wanted her
more.

His knees hit the bed and he dropped her onto the
soft surface. But before he could follow her down Hope

had already popped back up, her hands grappling with his fly.

Her fingers brushed the throbbing ridge of his erection. She tugged at the tab of his zipper. It went down a centimeter and then stopped. She jerked at it, up and down, metal grinding against metal, but it didn't budge.

Round, disbelieving eyes collided with his. "It's stuck."

Of course it was. The universe was conspiring against him, that was all there was to it.

He laughed. What else could he do? Gage grabbed her hands and fell to the bed with her lush body sprawled across him.

"This isn't funny," she exclaimed, staring down at him as if he was on the verge of losing his mind. Maybe he was.

"Yes...yes, it is. I finally get you naked and I can't get my damn pants off." He devolved into laughter again. It was either that or scream in frustration. Laughter was the saner response...but only just.

Hope didn't join him. Apparently she didn't see the humor. Instead, the sharp heels of her palms dug into his chest as she levered herself off of him so that she could study him with narrowed eyes. Her teeth tugged at her bottom lip, pulling it into her mouth. He wanted to do that, but considering his dick was currently being held hostage, that probably wasn't a good idea.

"How much do you like them?"

"Right now? Not at all."

"Good."

She crawled up his body and across the bed. He nearly groaned when her sex, still wet and swollen from the release he'd given her downstairs, hovered right above his face.

Dammit! Now *this* was torture. If the insurgents had dangled a willing and aroused Hope just out of his reach he might have told them whatever they wanted.

With a moan of surrender, even as he realized this agony would be self-inflicted, Gage surged up to taste her. A tremor rocked through her body and her hips bucked against his mouth.

"Gage," she cautioned, breathlessly, as something metallic clattered above his head. He was too preoccupied to puzzle out the source of the sound.

To his amusement, and disappointment, after several moments, Hope physically launched herself backward out of his hold. She knelt between his open knees, her breasts bobbing up and down with each labored breath and a gleaming pair of scissors clutched triumphantly in one hand and a condom in the other.

"Have I mentioned that you're amazing?" he asked. Folding his arms beneath his head, Gage held still and waited for her to start cutting.

"You might want to wait until they're off," she suggested, opening and closing the scissors with a metallic snick.

She wrapped a hand in his waistband again and pointed the scissors straight for his groin. "Uh," he started to protest, but thought better of whatever he was going to say. Better not to distract a woman with a sharp object that close to his cock.

In one clean snip a jagged line appeared beside his fly.

Finally. The relief—figuratively and literally—was

unbelievable. There was nothing left to prevent him from having Hope.

The scissors clattered to the floor, probably the safest place for them right now. Her hand plunged into the opening she'd created and wrapped around his aching sex. He gasped and nearly jackknifed off the bed. A purr of satisfaction rolled through her chest and echoed deep inside him.

She worked him, squeezing, stroking, driving him crazy. Her fingers slipped over the sensitive head of his cock, making his hips thrust and beg for more. Hell, if she kept doing that his pants wouldn't make it off before he exploded.

And that was not how this night was going to go. He'd waited too long for this for it to be over that quickly.

Grasping her wrist, he pulled her hand away. Her lips drew down into a deliciously tempting pout. He'd never been the kind of guy to like that sort of thing, but on Hope everything looked good.

Lifting his hips, he pushed the ruined jeans down his body. Hope realized what he wanted and helped.

He saw the gleam in her eyes. The way she stared at him and licked her lips. His cock jerked, wanting closer to that mouth. Oh, yeah, he was in trouble.

Executing preemptive maneuvers, Gage pulled her back to the bed and flattened her onto her stomach. He rose above her, his hand pressing gently into her spine to keep her exactly where he wanted…while he regained some equilibrium and much-needed control.

His mouth touched down onto the center of her back and she shivered. He trailed his tongue up the sensitive knots of her spine, relishing the taste and feel of her skin. Sweet. Hot. Perfect. Better than anything he'd ever imagined.

"Didn't you get enough of this downstairs?" Hope craned her neck around so that she could look at him.

He smiled wickedly against her skin, latching onto the nape of her neck and relishing the broken sound when she sucked in a breath. "Never."

He worked his way down again, nipping at the pale, round globes of her ass. She writhed beneath him. Her thighs fell open and he could smell the heady scent of her arousal. For him.

His hands followed the same path, urging her wider so that he could see all of her.

Downstairs he'd been hell-bent on making her scream as fast and hard as possible. He wasn't taking the chance that she would come to her senses and change her mind. Not without a taste of her.

Now that he knew she wasn't going to tell him to leave…he could take his time. And that's exactly what he intended to do.

His fingers slipped down the dent of her rear, following the path until he reached the slippery entrance to her sex. He hadn't taken the time to touch and explore. Now he did, learning all he could about her.

The way her body clenched when he pushed into her channel the slightest bit, trying to beckon him farther. The broken sound she made when his thumb pressed against her clit. The shiver of her body. The unconscious grind of her hips.

She buried her forehead against the bed when he plunged a finger deep inside her and strained back against the invasion, asking for more. Kneeling between her open thighs, he bent over and sucked gently on the tender bundle of nerves at the base of her spine. He worked his fingers in and out of her, slowly, steadily, driving them both crazy.

His own hips pumped in time to the thrust of his hand, wanting nothing more than to bury to the hilt deep inside her.

Not. Yet.

He had good intentions, but Hope took them all away. Surging away from him, she lunged across the bed, twisted and threw something at him. He caught the tiny square packet right before it hit his face. His battle-honed reflexes were the only thing that kept him from getting a corner in the eye.

"Now, Gage. Please," she begged, her beautifully naked body spread-eagled across the bed.

How could he deny her anything? Especially something he wanted so desperately himself.

Rolling the condom down over his aching erection, Gage grasped Hope's thighs and pulled her back to him. He didn't bother turning her over, but lifted her up onto her knees and drove deep inside her.

She let out a strangled sound. He stilled. She warned, "Don't you dare stop," with what little breath she still had.

He'd always been good at taking orders. Okay, that was a lie. But he'd gotten a hell of a lot better at it.

The walls of her sex held on to him, squeezing tight. She rolled her hips and he nearly lost it. His fingers bit into her, trying to keep her still. But neither of them could stand it.

Gage pulled slowly out and then sank back into her. He did it again, running a hand down her spine. Hope followed him, grinding back against him so that she could get more, taking everything.

Desperation swamped him. Touching her, having her, thrusting deep inside her felt so damn good. Gage ground his teeth together, trying to stretch this out and prolong the moment. But he'd wanted her way too long for that to last. His body had other ideas.

Pretty soon he was thrusting against her so hard and fast that he couldn't tell when one surge ended and another began. Hope panted. They both did. He couldn't catch his breath, but who cared about dying? Not him. Not now.

With one hand he held Hope's hips in place. The other pressed her shoulders tight to the bed. He could feel the tremors of her release tempting him to just let go. Every muscle in her body quivered, on the edge of something great.

He felt it, too. Knew what was coming. Together, they strained for release. And when it hit, it overwhelmed them both.

Hope's hands gripped the bed so tightly her knuckles turned white. Her mouth was locked open on a silent scream that her body was too busy to let free.

Gage didn't have that problem. The orgasm hit like a fist upside the head. A kaleidoscope of color flashed across his eyes. The room spun and he wasn't sure he was even still upright. The tight grip of Hope's sex clutched on to him, the only solid and certain thing.

Several minutes later the world righted itself and Gage realized Hope was pinned beneath his leaden body. At least he'd had the forethought to land half on and half off of her. Although, he could still feel the jerky hitch of an aftershock as it rumbled through her body.

After several minutes, she stirred, disentangling their limbs and shoving him away so she could flop bonelessly onto her back. For a second her callous treatment bothered him—casual sex had never concerned him before, but this was Hope—until she pulled his arm back over her hip and curled into him.

She buried her nose against his collarbone, and her soft words whispered against his skin. "Thank God I never knew you were that good. I might not have found the resolve to watch you go."

HOPE STRETCHED SLOWLY, a smile on her face before her eyes had even opened. Several places on her body protested, but she ignored them. Not even sore muscles could take away the contentment that effervesced through her.

The smell of frying bacon drifted up the stairs from the kitchen. She couldn't remember having bacon to cook.

Even though the tantalizing scent meant he couldn't be there beside her, Hope found herself reaching out and running her hand across the cool sheet where Gage should have been. The spot didn't have any residual body heat. How long had he been up?

And why did it bother her that he hadn't slept as soundly as she had?

A sharp sound reverberating from her front door prevented her from looking too closely at her reaction. Nothing good could come from it, anyway.

Grabbing a robe off the back of her bathroom door, Hope padded down the stairs on bare feet. Her hand was inches away from the knob when Gage appeared beside the banister, a spatula hanging loosely in his hand.

"I wouldn't do that if I were you."

Hope froze. He looked amazing. His chest was bare and the jeans he'd thrown on rode low on his hips. *Where the hell had they come from?* He hadn't bothered to zip or snap them, which made Hope seriously consider how easy it would be to get him back out of them.

Another knock pounded on the door behind her.

Frowning, she spun away to glare at the thing. She took a single step toward it. Shaking his head, Gage said, "Suit yourself," and then turned back to the kitchen.

Bypassing the door, Hope headed for the window that ran beside it so that she could see who was assaulting her door this early in the morning. And was shocked at the sight that greeted her.

There was no sign of the bike Gage had parked at the curb yesterday when they'd driven home in the rain. Instead, a handful of news trucks occupied the space, their satellite antennas stretching high against the bright blue sky.

There must have been fifteen or twenty people milling around on her front lawn. Women in suits and full makeup. Men in ties and fancy dress shoes. Almost all of them had paper coffee cups from the diner clutched in their hands.

"What the hell," she exclaimed. Several people closest to the house turned to look at her—apparently she needed to get thicker windows, not that soundproofing had been a real issue before today. Several of them leaped into action, grabbing up cameras and snapping off several pictures before she had a chance to duck back behind the door.

"I told you," Gage hollered from the safety of her kitchen.

Careful not to walk in front of the windows, Hope headed into the back of the house.

"What is going on?" she demanded, stopping just inside the room and crossing her arms over her chest.

Gage, standing at her stove, the handle of her skillet in one hand and the spatula in the other, tossed a frown at her over his shoulder. "I'm making omelets. Do you want bacon or veggie?"

"I don't want either!"

"Breakfast is the most important meal of the day, Hope." Tigger wound in a figure eight between his open feet.

"I want to know what those people are doing on my front lawn."

"I'd think that was obvious. Especially for someone who works at a newspaper. They're waiting for a story."

Frustration jangled through her. "But why do they expect to find one here?" she asked slowly, hoping eventually she'd hit on the right question to ask him so that she'd get some answers.

He shrugged. "You'd know that better than I would."

"What exactly is that supposed to mean?" she asked, a dangerous edge creeping into her voice.

"Well, I didn't stop long enough to ask them, Hope. I didn't think that would be smart. My guess is that someone tipped them off that I was over here." He eyed her with speculation.

"You think I called them?" Incredulity made her voice squeak. She cleared it away, irritated with herself. "Why in God's name would I do that?"

"I don't know. You tell me."

She wouldn't, for a number of reasons, but the most important one being the people currently camped out on her front lawn were the *competition*. Just thinking the word made a sharp pain lance through her belly. No, she would not feel guilty about this! She hadn't done anything wrong. She had not called them.

Gage's jaw muscles rippled. Apparently he decided her silence was as good as admission.

"You're the only person who knew I was here."

"Not true," Hope answered slowly. "Willow knew exactly what was going to happen when we left that bowling alley."

"So you think your friend sold you out?"

"No!" Hope yelled, throwing her hands up with annoyance. "But all it would have taken was an innocent comment to explain why we'd left and everyone within hearing distance probably jumped to the same conclusion. Besides, your bike was parked outside my house all night. You know how efficient the Sweetheart grapevine is. Everyone in town probably knew you were staying the night before we'd even made it upstairs to the bed."

Gage hummed in the back of his throat. "True."

"God, I really hate this town."

He threw her a skeptical glance.

"Sometimes. Most of the time."

"Then why are you still here?"

"It's complicated."

"No, it isn't, Hope. I know you, probably better than just about anyone."

"You knew me. Past tense."

He shrugged. "You're stubborn. Once you've made

up your mind nothing can change it. If you wanted out of here you'd already be gone."

"My dad was sick."

"And now he isn't."

"I've taken over so much at the paper."

"Which you could walk away from tomorrow. There are other employees, right?"

"Yes, but none of them are family. That's my heritage."

"Which you don't want." A single eyebrow quirked up in a condescending arch. "Lip service, that's all it is. If you ask me, you don't really want to leave Sweetheart."

Hope's eyes widened. A nasty knot of sludgy emotions filled her belly. Suddenly, she wasn't very hungry.

She opened her mouth to snarl at him about the article she was going to write—her ticket out of here—but realized she couldn't rub it in his face without tipping her hand.

The article she hadn't even made an attempt to work on since they'd been paired together. He was right. What had happened to her resolve? Apparently it had been trumped by her wayward libido.

Maybe now that her lust had been slaked perhaps she could focus.

Gage shifted at her stove, flashing a glimpse of the open V at his hips. The chain reaction through her body was immediate and depressingly obvious. Her knees trembled.

Giving him her back, Hope called him every derogatory name she could think of beneath her breath. And the idiot had the audacity to grin knowingly at her. He was playing dirty.

The mischievously sexy grin made her heart flip-flop.

Which only made her angrier—with herself. He'd been home how many days? And not only had she let him into her bed, but she'd also let him worm his way back into her life. Her attraction to him was clouding her judgment and distracting her from the plan.

Another knock reverberated through her front hall. It was the catalyst that sent her sailing over the edge of civility.

The vultures on her front stoop had gone too far. They'd cast a pall over the night that she and Gage had just shared and they were trying to horn in on *her* story.

Hope headed for the fireplace at the far end of her living room. Above the rough-hewn beam that served as her mantel, the shotgun her great-grandpa had used to defend his land almost one hundred years ago hung in the place of honor.

It was an heirloom, and while it had once been a fine piece of weaponry, it hadn't been shot in at least forty years. But the people on her front lawn didn't know that. Worse, they were so obviously city types that they probably wouldn't be able to tell the difference between a museum-quality rifle and one that could shoot buckshot into their backsides.

At least that's what she was hoping for.

Scraping the hair back from her forehead, she thought about throwing some clothes on, but decided if she did she might lose her momentum.

Hope stalked to the front door, snatched the knob and yanked it open. As one, the twenty-odd people on her front lawn turned to stare at her.

"Oh, hell," Gage said from behind her.

She shot a glare at him over her shoulder, hoping the

heat in her eyes was all the warning he needed to stay put. The last thing she wanted was for him to walk out behind her half-naked and blunt the impact of her gun.

She grasped the rifle in both hands just as her daddy had taught her. She might not have ever needed to shoot a gun, but every good Southern girl worth her salt at least knew how. The woods that bordered the town were full of dangerous animals—cougars, bears, coyotes, bobcats.

"This is private property. You have exactly ninety seconds to clear out before I start shooting."

"Come on, Ms. Rawlings, you're one of us," a voice yelled from the back of the group.

She smiled, baring her teeth in an unfriendly snarl that probably resembled one of the animals her skills were supposed to defend against. "No, I'm not. I'm a journalist, not a vulture happy to pick through the scraps of someone's misfortune. Now, just to be fair, I should probably point out that the sheriff is my godfather and if I tell him I was afraid the mob on my front lawn was about to turn rabid he's likely to believe me."

To prove her point, Hope raised the rifle to her shoulder, closed one eye and sighted down the barrel, picking out a man in the back of the pack to aim at. If the rifle had actually been loaded she never would have done that, but since she didn't even own bullets for the damn thing...

The bluff worked and everyone scattered. She was actually impressed at how quickly they could move. Unfortunately, several of them paused long enough to snap a photograph. She'd probably regret this when she appeared in a newspaper or online somewhere. She could already see the headline—Crazed Local Journalist Threatens First Amendment with a Rifle.

When she was certain they were all leaving Hope walked back inside, closed the door and then sagged heavily against it.

"Hell."

Gage stood there, two plates in his hands, and stared at her across the space.

"You're remarkable, you know that?"

10

"REMIND ME AGAIN, why are we doing this?" Gage asked, stalking up the walk to his sister's store hot on Hope's heels. He had no desire to eat dinner with his sister and the guy she'd been paired with.

Not when he could have had Hope flat on her back in bed. After the incident on her front lawn, they'd come to an uneasy truce. Neither of them mentioned anything likely to require her to pull that gun out again and he got to kiss and touch her as much as he wanted.

"Because Lexi asked us to meet Brandon."

"Why? She's known the guy for less than three days."

Hope paused, her fingers wrapped around the door handle. She swept him with a warning look that was probably supposed to shrink his balls to an appropriately cowed size, but really only made him want to kiss her senseless.

She was so cute when she was trying to be fierce. And if he hadn't been tortured by some of the best in the business the glance might have actually worked.

"What difference does that make? You've only been

home for a handful of days and look at how quickly you made it to home plate."

"That's different," Gage growled. The thought of anyone—especially a stranger—doing to Lexi what he'd done to Hope last night…didn't sit well. At all. "We've known each other for years."

A shadow passed across her eyes, dulling the glitter in the green-gold depths. "Have we?" she asked, pulling open the door and rushing inside.

He grasped her arm and pulled her around to look at him. But she wouldn't meet his eyes. "What the heck is that supposed to mean?"

"Gage. Hope." Lexi popped up from the back of the store, interrupting. Gage sent her a warning glance, but either she didn't see it or ignored it. Neither option made him happy.

His sister rushed around the counter and hugged Hope. She whispered something into her ear that had Hope dissolving into laughter.

Turning to him, Lexi gave him the same hug, but instead of whispering in his ear she pulled back, glared at him and said, "You had better behave."

Hope smothered a snort. "I think that's a lost cause, Lexi. When has Gage ever done what he's told?"

"Never." His sister sighed.

Gage split his focus between the two of them, waited for a beat and then headed for the door. "I don't have to take this shit."

Lexi grabbed one arm. Hope grasped the other. They both tugged at him. He relentlessly drove toward the door, anyway, dragging them behind him.

"She's sorry. Say you're sorry, Lexi," Hope prompted, her voice full of checked humor.

"I'm sorry," his sister said, contrition filling the words. But her eyelids dropped to conceal the telltale glitter behind them.

"Sure you are."

The bell above the door jangled. All three of them glanced up at the man standing just inside the doorway.

Lexi dropped his arm as if she'd been burned and ran a hand over her hair.

The man's gaze, way more calculating than Gage liked, took in the entire scene. "I could come back later."

"Don't you dare." Lexi shot forward, grabbed his hand and pulled him farther into the front of her store. "Gage was just being an idiot, as usual."

His sister brought the other man over and made the introductions. "Brandon, this is my brother, Gage, and his date, Hope. This is Brandon. He's a nurse in Hilton Head."

"Nice to meet you," Gage grunted, narrowing his eyes as he studied the other man. He didn't look like any nurse Gage had ever met.

Brandon answered him stare for stare, refusing to flinch. If they'd been anywhere else Gage might have given him points for taking him on, but there was something about him…

Hope, apparently sensing the impending danger even if Lexi didn't, stepped up beside him. She placed a cool hand on his arm. "Lexi, is there anything Gage and I can help with in the kitchen?"

"Absolutely not. Y'all have a seat." Lexi waved her hands at a table on the far side of the room that she'd set for four. Several rosebuds—probably from Petals—sat in a small vase next to drippy candles she'd placed in an old wine bottle.

The three of them moved to sit, but Lexi stopped her date. "Brandon, could you help me?"

Gage froze halfway to his seat and immediately began to reverse directions. Hope stopped him and softly murmured, "Let him go."

He glared at Brandon's back as the two of them disappeared behind the red-and-white-checkered curtain. When the object of his ire was gone, he switched the glare to Hope.

Her mouth was pulled straight into a serious line, but her eyes shimmered with amusement.

"I don't like him."

She nodded solemnly, the agreeable gesture at odds with the sarcastic tone of her voice. "Really," she drawled. "Would you like anyone your sister was dating?"

"Of course. She's dated before and I didn't have any problem with the guys. It's him…" His voice trailed off as Hope shook her head.

"She was what, twelve, when you left?"

Gage nodded, trying to see the minefield she was laying for him with the question. Instinct told him it was there, he just hadn't found it yet.

"Not exactly dating then, was she?"

He shook his head, finally seeing where Hope was going with this and not liking it one bit.

"Give me some credit. I know she's an adult. A perfectly intelligent woman capable of taking care of herself. But…"

Hope leaned across the table. She set both of her hands on either side of his face and brought them close. She stared into his eyes for several seconds before saying, "It's sweet. How much you care about her and want to protect her. I wish I had an older brother who cared about me that way." Then she pressed her mouth to his.

The kiss was soft, soothing, although that ever-present lick of need still managed to whip through him.

She pulled back, but instead of letting her, Gage wrapped his hands around her arms and held her there. "I distinctly remember you saying something about thinking of me as a brother."

Her lips pulled down at the corners. Gage leaned forward and touched his mouth to them. "I lied," she mumbled against him.

"No, really?"

A cough sounded from across the room. He glanced over her shoulder to find his sister standing there, both hands full of serving platters. Behind her, Brandon watched. The back of Gage's neck tightened and tingled a warning.

The last time he'd ignored the sensation he and several of his friends had ended up in a shitload of trouble. He had no intention of ignoring it again.

The dinner was nice. Lexi was a fantastic cook and her talents went much further than candy and chocolate. Watching Gage and Brandon dance around each other might have been amusing if she hadn't been on constant alert for a sign that it was getting out of control.

Gage had been…on edge all night. At first she'd thought it was just the in-your-face reality of his sister dating. But it was more than that.

She could feel the buzz of energy running through him. The charge had transferred to her when their skin touched. And it wasn't pleasure.

His eyes were watchful and hyperaware, taking in

every detail around them. There'd been a hardness in the golden-brown depths—still was twenty minutes after they'd left and were settled into the comfort of her living room.

Hope had purposely changed into something comfortable and made them both a warm cup of tea while Gage lit a fire. She wasn't sure how to take it that he hadn't immediately tried to get her into bed when they'd walked in the door.

Part of her was relieved, because in his current mood, she wasn't sure she'd have been up for that. He obviously had something on his mind and she didn't want to be the nameless, faceless distraction he used to ignore it.

Tucking her bare feet beneath her, she curled up into the armchair directly across from the fireplace. Gage crouched in front of it, poker in hand, and stared at the fledgling flames, ignoring the cup she'd placed on the hearth beside him.

How easy it had been to fall straight back into the comfort of their past friendship. It was almost as if those twelve years, and that final fight, had never happened. Although, even if they hadn't mentioned it, both of them remembered.

"Want to tell me what's wrong?"

Gage glanced over his shoulder and then, with a steady grace that always managed to surprise her, stood. "Nothing's wrong."

"Now who's lying?"

His jaw flexed and his molars ground together. He glared at her, but didn't argue the point. They both knew she was right.

"Are you still worried about your sister dating Brandon?"

"Yes."

But even as he said the word Hope knew that wasn't the real problem. His mixed emotions over that might not be helping, but the surly, bottled-up anger went deeper than that.

"Is it what happened in Afghanistan?" she asked slowly. Part of her wanted him to say no. She wasn't sure she could deal with the details if he decided to open up. What he'd been through...her imagination had filled in enough blanks and nothing she'd come up with had been good.

"No."

She should have felt relief, but she didn't. "Then what, Gage? Talk to me."

A bitter sound erupted from his throat. Rubbing his hands over his face, Gage sank onto the sofa.

Neither of them had bothered to turn the lights on. Firelight flickered, but it wasn't enough to let her see the expression on his face.

And she wanted to see him. To help him. To solve whatever had tightened his shoulders with unforgiving stiffness. She hadn't seen him this...tense since the night of the cocktail party.

Slowly, she rose from her chair and transferred to the cushion beside him. Her arm brushed against his shoulder. She tried not to let it hurt when he shifted away from her, but it was difficult to stifle the reaction. Of course it hurt.

She didn't want it to, but what was it Jenna had said? Oh, yeah. Not *wanting* to care and not caring weren't the same thing.

Boy did she understand what her friend had meant. She hated to see anyone so tied up in knots. Especially someone as brave, protective and honorable as Gage.

Finding the strength to push through, she laid her hand on his thigh, bracing to be rebuffed again. But he didn't move away this time.

"Tell me."

"No."

She grasped his chin and made him look at her. "Tell me."

"No," he growled, fire and anger and bitterness staring back at her. "Let it go, Hope. This has nothing to do with you."

She narrowed her own eyes. Part of her begged to coddle him. To stroke his hair and kiss his lips and promise him whatever was wrong would be okay. But he'd hate that. And it wouldn't get either of them anywhere.

It certainly wouldn't help him.

So she stuffed down her own protective instincts and decided to fight fire with fire.

"This doesn't have anything to do with me? Just a few days ago you showed up on my doorstep in the middle of the night. Sadness, guilt and dread exhausting you to the point of collapse. You didn't keep that to yourself, you self-righteous bastard."

A snarl curled his lips. In one surge he had her flat on her back. She hadn't even had time to brace for the impact...but maybe that was better.

She could see it, that wild, reckless passion that had always scared her, filling him up. It flushed his sun-tinged skin, glowed at her from flashing eyes and crushed her beneath the weight of what she'd goaded from him.

For the space of a heartbeat she wondered if she'd gone too far. And then his mouth crushed hers and she didn't care. His hands ripped at her clothes, fighting to find bare skin. His lips punished her, sucking the blood to the surface of her skin and leaving marks she'd wear tomorrow.

And the whole time he argued with himself—and her.

"Do you think I want you to know what I've done? That I've killed men?"

"Only in self-defense," she argued, holding onto him because he was the only solid thing around her.

"You don't know that."

"I do."

His mouth latched onto her shoulder. She expected the draw as he tugged on her skin, but it never came. Instead, the soft edge of his tongue brushed against her.

And she knew the anger he'd been using as a shield was gone.

"I've seen terrible things," he said, his voice shaking slightly. With anyone else she probably wouldn't have even noticed the miniscule sign of vulnerability, but she was so attuned to him now…there was no way she could have missed it.

"But I refuse to tell you about them. I don't want to relive the memories. All I want to do is forget."

His hot mouth traveled up the sharp edge of her collarbone. "Try to forget," he whispered.

And her heart broke. The damn thing just cracked wide-open. She'd been holding it closed with everything she had, but it wasn't enough. Not when the strong, honorable man he'd become was this damaged.

His mouth played across her skin. His fingers pulled at the neckline of her shirt, exposing more of her that he could taste. The frenzy of anger had left him, but she almost wished for it back.

That she could deal with. This…she wasn't sure. Not and keep herself protected, anyway.

Gage pulled back. He stared down at her with cloudy, shadowed eyes. "I don't want it to touch you, Hope. Ever. You or Lexi or my mom and dad."

"But it does. It touches all of them because it touches you."

He pressed his forehead against hers. "But I don't want it to."

Hope kissed him. She didn't know what else to do. How else to get through to him. He was so damn strong, her soldier.

No, he wasn't hers. At least not past tonight. Or tomorrow. Or this week. But for now that was enough.

Touching him was enough.

Why hadn't she realized that so much sooner?

Hope opened for him, spreading her lips and thighs and soul wide so that he could have a soft place to land.

Last night had been all about the rush. The first discovery of each other. This time—now—was all about savoring.

Her toes dug into the end of the sofa, giving her purchase so she could rub against him. She luxuriated in the sensation. The drag of his body against hers. The rough abrasion of cloth and skin. Her eyes slid closed and she just felt.

The experience swamped her, filled every sense. The

taste of his lips against her mouth. The chocolate they'd had for dessert and the bitter tang of strong black coffee. The scent of both mixed with the wild spice of arousal—his and hers.

His breath soughed softly against her. The fire crackled and popped. She wanted to feel the warmth of it mixed with him against her skin.

Her hands curled over his shoulders and she pushed against him. Immediately Gage moved away, putting space between them. He stared down at her, his pupils dark and open with longing.

"What's wrong?"

"Not a thing," she promised, scooting out from under him, anyway.

Slowly, she stood and turned her back to the fireplace. Gage started to follow her, but she shook her head and he stilled.

Heat seeped beneath the layer of her clothes. Too warm. Even for the thin lounging pants and matching emerald-green top she'd thrown on.

Crossing her arms over her chest, Hope reached for the hem and in one smooth motion yanked the shirt off over her head. Her hair rained back down around her and she shook it impatiently out of her face. She wanted to see his expression.

And she wasn't disappointed. He watched her with sharp, calculating eyes, tracking even the slightest twitch.

She hadn't bothered putting on a bra, or panties, although he hadn't realized that just yet. After being constricted all night by the outfit she'd chosen, it had felt fantastic to just be.

And liberating that she could be that way with Gage.

She started to push the pants off of her hips, but before she could he stopped her. His fingers clamped over hers, stilling her.

Somewhere between the couch and her spot in front of the fire he yanked his own shirt over his head. With one hand he held both of hers. The other swept the curling ends of her hair over her shoulder so that they fell down her back.

Orange, gold and red light flicked across his skin. She'd been so frenzied last night that she hadn't noticed the tiny jagged lines that crisscrossed his stomach.

Hope ran her fingers across them, surprised to feel the skin smooth except for the coarse hair sprinkled over his chest and abs. She wanted to bend down and press her mouth to each and every one of the scars.

Instead, Gage pulled her tight against him. Her breasts flattened to his chest. The rough hair teased her already-distended nipples, making them ache. His hands brushed down the length of her spine, disappearing beneath the forgiving waistband of her pants to cup the heavy curve of her rear.

He filled his palms with her, using the grip to boost her harder against him. His fingers flexed and dipped into the dent between her cheeks. The barest hint of his fingertips caressed the damp swirl of her sex.

She gasped and arched against him. With nothing more than a flex of his wrists, her pants slid down her thighs to pool at her feet, leaving her clothed in nothing but an iridescent glow.

He kissed her. Devoured her. Her spine arched backward beneath the onslaught of his desire. But it still wasn't enough. She wanted more. Throbbed with a deep need for more.

Gage broke away from her, grabbed a pillow from the couch and threw it to the floor at her feet. He dropped to his knees and tugged her down with him. Cupping her head in his huge hands, he guided her down to the floor and the waiting cushion.

She burned. Not from the fire, but from him. He stretched out beside her, the perfect backstop to bounce and deflect the warmth straight back at her.

With a single fingertip, he ran it from her temple behind her ear, across the hollow at the base of her throat, through the valley between her breasts, over her ribs, across a hip, along the outside of her thigh, to the peak of her knee and shin to the very tip of her toes. The caress was soft. It tickled. Hot, smoldering eyes followed the path, taking in every naked, accessible inch that he'd touched.

Hope was suddenly self-conscious. She'd never been before, but with Gage… He saw way too much. She almost wished for the frenzy. That mindless need was a shield, a protective wall she could hide behind.

Without a single word he'd stripped that away from her and laid her absolutely bare.

Hope moved to cover herself. It was way too late for the gesture, but she needed to do something.

Her palm covered the juncture of her thighs.

His thumb and forefinger wrapped around her wrist, his hand so large the fingers overlapped. "Don't," he admonished, gently tugging her away.

A buzz of annoyance shot through her.

"Why do you get to avoid me, but I can't avoid you?"

A smile tugged at his mouth, pulling it into a lopsided grin. "Let's just say it's your turn. Do you know how much courage it took to ask you out even when you obviously thought it was a joke? How much it hurt every time you said no?"

"Please," she scoffed. "If it bothered you so much why did you keep asking?"

He leaned over and pressed his open mouth to her shoulder. "The possibility of you saying yes was more important than the reality of you saying no."

His body covered hers and she let him, any thought of protecting herself evaporating away like the smoke disappearing up the chimney. He seduced her with soft words and teasing kisses.

Last night they'd come together in a conflagration of need. Tonight was different. More.

Gage touched her everywhere. He parted her thighs and claimed her as his. He left his mark not just on her skin but deep inside where no one but she could see.

Somewhere along the way his pants disappeared and a condom appeared. Wrapping an arm beneath her leg, he pushed her knee up and out, opening her to him.

With slow, sure strokes, he brought them together. He settled deep inside her, filling her as nothing and no one else ever had. She could feel him straight through to the center of her soul.

Together they found a rhythm, rocking back and forth together to prolong the pleasure of each other. His mouth and hands touched her everywhere, stoking the blaze inside her higher. The pressure built, a steady climb to the highest peak.

In and out, Gage buried his face in the crook of her neck. His fingers tightened at her hips. She gripped his shoulders, searching for purchase in the middle of the relentless surrender.

The first ripple of release surged through her, taking her by surprise because it came out of nowhere. A sound caught in the back of her throat. But Gage wasn't through. He kept pushing her, demanding that she give him more. Give him everything.

And she couldn't say no. Couldn't have stopped him even if she'd wanted to.

The pressure built again, an overwhelming band of tension and need. It didn't take long to snap again, her entire body quivering.

But he still wasn't through. Gage kept going, showing her that this was just the beginning. She was certain each peak he drove her to was the last she could possibly take. And each time she was wrong. There was always more.

Hope lost track of how many times she came. Two, three, six. They were just numbers and didn't actually mean anything.

Her head thrashed against the floor, the pillow long gone. Her fingernails raked down his back, possibly peeling skin. Every muscle in her body throbbed and sobbed and shook. She was exhausted and energized. Her throat was so sore from screaming his name that she'd given up saying anything.

All she could do was feel.

At last he joined her. It was Hope's turn to surge against him, crashing them together over and over again. His hands grasped her face, holding her steady. His eyelids flickered, but he refused to break the connection as he stared straight into the center of her.

She felt the kick of his release deep inside her. The surge of him sent her over the edge one last time. Her muscles were a quivering mass of jelly, but somehow she found the strength to wrap her thighs around him, holding him tight against her.

Together, they collapsed to the floor in the aftermath.

Sweat glistened across their skin, gleaming in the firelight.

Hope wanted to say something, but she had no idea what. And really, she'd already done enough.

He'd done exactly what she'd always been afraid of— made her care. And unlike before, she'd done nothing to protect herself.

11

THE PHONE ON HOPE'S desk rang. She wasn't happy. It had taken her a while to get into the rhythm of work…she kept thinking about last night with Gage. And every time she did, something fluttered uncomfortably inside her chest.

Tasks that should have taken her a few minutes were requiring hours. She wanted desperately to get some writing in, but all the paperwork, organization and delegation were getting in the way. She'd assigned a handful of pieces to their writing staff, jealous of every one. But she couldn't spare the time right now to take any for herself.

Ripping the offending interruption off the cradle, Hope ground out, "Hope Rawlings, *Sweetheart Sentinel*," and hoped that whoever was calling wouldn't add to her to-do list.

"Ms. Rawlings." It was the smooth, deep voice of the managing editor from the *Atlanta Courier*. Hope immediately straightened in her chair. Guilt, hope and dread all blended into a poisonous mix.

"Mr. Rebman, what can I do for you?"

"I hear you've become rather close with Gage Harper in the last few days. I was hoping that meant you'd have a piece for me soon. If so, I'd like to run it on Wednesday."

Hope sputtered. "How...what...?" Wednesday was Valentine's Day. Why would he want to run a piece about the capture and torture of a soldier on Valentine's Day? She'd had the *Sweetheart Sentinel*'s Valentine's Day edition planned for weeks. Full of heartwarming fluff pieces.

The timing struck her as wrong.

"Wednesday? Why tomorrow?"

"According to my sources, the piece you're writing should fit perfectly as the headline feature for our Valentine's edition. Scarred soldier returns from a harrowing experience, rekindles old flame with a woman he hasn't seen for years and ends up happily ever after."

Silence buzzed down the line. She had no idea how to respond to that, but the sinking sensation in her stomach didn't think it was a good idea at all.

"This gives me the best of both worlds, Ms. Rawlings. Exclusive content about one of the most sought-after stories and a warm, fuzzy, hearts-and-flowers ending on the most romantic day of the year. Any possibility he's going to ask you to marry him?"

"No!" Hope jumped out of her chair, her heart racing painfully in her chest. She modulated her voice and answered again. "No."

"Too bad, but I suppose it is a little quick. We'll spin it to give the impression that outcome is inevitable."

The hell they would. Anger—where had it been

before now?—suffused her, sending a ripple of heat through her.

Reaching behind her, Hope grabbed her chair and carefully sank into it.

"Sources. You said you had sources. Who are they?"

"One of our brightest writers has been in Sweetheart for days." The man cackled. "Get this, somehow he's managed to convince Gage Harper's sister to talk to him. Something about Cupid or couples. I didn't get it. I don't care how he's doing it, but the girl has been spilling her guts for days. Intimate details about their family, how their father was hard on him growing up. Until he told me you had an in with Gage himself, I thought Brandon's position was genius."

Rage blinded her. Her hand gripped the edge of the phone so tightly she was surprised it didn't crumble to pieces.

"I have to admit, you surprised me, Ms. Rawlings. I honestly didn't think you had it in you to get the job done. Journalism can be a dirty business. You didn't strike me as ruthless enough."

Oh, she could be ruthless all right. And Brandon was about to figure out just how much.

Hope had no recollection of ending the call. She could have offered Mr. Rebman her firstborn child and she wouldn't remember. Her brain had been spinning with options on how to handle the situation.

She was going to have to tell Lexi. And Gage.

"Crap." Hope dropped her head into her hands. How was she supposed to do that without revealing how she'd gotten the information? Without telling them both that *she* was supposed to be writing a story about Gage.

It wasn't the same.

Yes, she'd maneuvered things so that she could be paired with Gage, but...she hadn't exactly done anything to get the story, had she? What little he had told her she wouldn't have been able to use, not without talking to him about it first.

And that was the difference between her and Brandon. Yes, she'd manipulated the situation for her own purposes, but she'd never intended to be truly underhanded. She'd always meant to convince him to give her the story, not steal it from him without his knowledge.

Hope rubbed her palms against tired, gritty eyes. Suddenly, she was exhausted. She hadn't exactly been spending the past few nights sleeping. Just thinking about how she'd left Gage this morning, mumbling grumpily into her pillow, made her insides turn to hot, achy goo.

God, she didn't want to tell him about Brandon. She knew he wouldn't handle it well. Obviously, she'd have to tell Lexi. And for a brief moment she fantasized about just telling her friend and leaving Gage completely out of it. But then the wary way he'd watched Brandon the previous night at dinner surfaced and she realized this wasn't information she could keep from him.

He deserved to know he'd been right about the other man.

But she'd definitely tell Lexi first.

At least that was the plan until soft lips pressed against the fingers covering her eyes.

"Rough day?" his warm voice asked.

Hope bolted upright in her chair and nearly cracked her forehead against his chin.

Gage stumbled backward, his hips landing on the

edge of her desk. "I'm sorry. I didn't mean to startle you."

A bouquet of flowers hung by his side. She knew from the pretty cellophane wrapping that he'd picked them up at Petals. And since four huge stargazer lilies— her favorite—dominated the bright bouquet, she knew Tatum had been fully aware they were meant for her.

And that she approved of Gage. If she hadn't then her friend would have sent him in here with a handful of red roses—the flower that required no imagination.

Hope's chest tightened. It took a lot to win over Tatum.

"Oh, hell," she breathed out, staring at the happy flowers bouncing back at her.

Following her glance, Gage held them out to her.

Slowly, she dropped her hands to her lap, then sat on them and looked up at Gage with wide, beseeching eyes.

"What is wrong with you, woman?" Gage grunted, reaching for her hand and hauling it out from beneath her. The long, thin wire-wrapped stems were stiff against her palm when he pried her fingers open and shoved the bouquet into her hand. "I think it's a little late to start that 'no' crap again, don't you?"

Not if she wanted to keep any part of herself safe and protected. Sex she could handle. Sex with him was rough and wild. For those few hours she could be reckless right along with him.

Flowers were…not wild. Too sweet. Just the cloyingly thick scent of them made her chest ache. Terribly.

She opened her mouth to say thank you. But the words wouldn't come. Not past the tight lump in her throat.

"Tell me what's bothering you," Gage demanded in a hard voice.

Oh, shit. How could she explain that she didn't want him to be romantic? That she could handle this—whatever this was—as long as she kept some distance between them. Last night had cut too damn close. But she could handle that. Somewhere in the light of day she'd convinced herself what had happened was nothing new. She'd always cared about Gage. So they'd added sex to the mix. They were both adults. It was hormones. Biology. Nothing more.

Flowers. His lopsided smile. Popping in unannounced at her office. Those were part of something they didn't have. Couldn't have.

She must have looked dumbfounded because he pressed her. "Why were you rubbing your eyes? Do you have a headache? Did something happen?"

Yes! She grabbed desperately at the excuse. "I had a phone call."

"Okay," he said slowly. "Everything okay with your dad?"

She waved away the conclusion he'd jumped to, but not before noticing that his first concern had immediately been her family. "As far as I know. No, this had nothing to do with me. Actually, it was about you. And Lexi."

Gage's eyes clouded with confusion.

Hope sucked in a deep breath. Stalling, she leaned forward and straightened the file folders spread across her desk so they were perfectly in line.

"For God's sake, just tell me."

"Brandon isn't a nurse. He's a reporter for the *Atlanta Courier*."

"What?" Gage vaulted away from her desk. Every muscle in his body tightened. His hands fisted, the white bandages glaringly obvious. "He lied."

"Apparently," she said dryly.

He stared at her, his eyes dangerously dark. She'd never seen him this...quiet and deadly. This was not good.

"Where is he?"

"How should I know?"

"You know everything that happens in this town, Hope. Find him. Now."

Her back stiffened. She resented being ordered around like some private. "We are not on a battlefield," she growled. "You might want to temper your authority issues and try again."

He squared off with her. Before, even though she could see it, all the seething energy that was clamoring for an outlet had been directed at someone else. Now it was pointed straight at her. And she didn't like it.

His jaw was so stiff she could have cracked pecans on it. His hand whipped out and ripped the flowers from her hand. She'd forgotten she was still holding them. Cellophane crinkled accusingly.

"Never mind."

He stalked out into the hallway. Her heart kicked hard against her ribs. She could have stayed there and let him go, but she didn't. Instead, she snatched up her cell phone and started dialing. "Lexi, where's Brandon?"

She shot into the hallway. "Damn, he's fast," she breathed when she realized he was already halfway across the bullpen to the back door. Dread bubbled through her blood.

"Here with me," Lexi answered.

Gage's palm hit the door with a metallic thud. Every pair of eyes in the place popped up to watch him stride angrily out the door, strangling a bouquet of flowers between his fingers.

Great. Everyone in town was going to think she'd just sent him packing.

"Tell him to run," Hope yelled into the phone, not bothering to wait to hear her response.

Two things became crystal clear. First, she'd never catch up to Gage with these damn heels on. Hope didn't even pause, but flicked her ankles and let each shoe clunk against the wall and fall drunkenly to the floor.

Second, Gage was going to kill someone.

"Call Sheriff Grant and tell him to go to Sugar and Spice right now," she said to Erica as she breezed past her cubicle.

The alarm at Sugar & Spice beeped a warning when Gage opened the back door. From the alley Hope could hear Lexi's confused exclamation. And the sickening thud of flesh on flesh.

Here they went again. Hope sighed. Was it only several days ago that she'd watched him let that guy beat the crap out of him? Brandon's image swam across her brain. Poor guy didn't stand a chance. At least the gym rat had known what he was getting into.

Not that she had much sympathy for Brandon. She just didn't want him to press charges. Or write an exposé on Gage going berserk.

Hope ignored the bite of pebbles against her bare feet. She raced inside in time to see Lexi standing between the two men. Blood flowed down Brandon's face from his already-swollen nose. Gage was trying to move Lexi out of the way, but she was fighting him.

Every time Gage found an inch, Brandon, coward that he was, would scoot back behind Lexi, perfectly content to use her as a human shield. Hope really didn't like the bastard.

"Lexi, get out of the way," Gage growled.

"Not until you tell me what's wrong." Lexi shot her a wild-eyed glance. "Hope, help me."

"As much as I abhor physical violence, trust me, he deserves whatever Gage wants to do to him."

"But—" Lexi began.

Hope cut her off. "However, you staying right where you are is probably the best way to keep your brother out of jail for murder."

Brandon's eyes widened to the size of silver dollars.

"Or maybe just assault with a deadly weapon."

"He doesn't have a weapon," Lexi cried.

"Have you seen his biceps and thighs? Trust me, the man is always packing." A shudder that had nothing to do with dread raced down her spine. Damn desire. Such inappropriate timing.

The dark glare that Gage sent her said he knew exactly what thought had crossed her mind and didn't like the timing, either.

Hmm...maybe she could use that. Channel that aggression down another avenue.

Gage reached over Lexi's shoulder and grasped Brandon's collar. He gathered the material into his fist and squeezed. The other man's skin turned bright red and his chest rose and fell on strangled breaths. Gage wasn't holding onto him that hard...it was pure adrenaline-fueled terror that had him close to hyperventilating.

"This as— Prick lied to you, Lexi. He's a reporter."

"What?" Her friend spun between the two men.

"He's using you to get to me."

"Is that true?" Lexi asked, her tone every bit as harsh as Gage's now.

"No."

Hope snorted. Gage growled. The man changed his mind about keeping up the lie. "Yes, I'm a reporter."

She'd never seen her friend ready to kill. But the way she leaped up off the floor and went straight for his throat... Apparently bloodthirstiness ran in the family. Not that she blamed Lexi. If the situation didn't require someone to keep a level head, she might have been in the thick of things right with them.

Gage strangled a startled laugh. Before Lexi's hands could connect, his strong arm wrapped around her waist and hauled her backward. Lexi flailed for several seconds before coming to the conclusion that she couldn't fight Gage's strength. Who could?

She stilled, her arms and legs dangling like loose, useless noodles, Gage's arm and hip keeping her off the floor. With as much dignity as that position would allow, she ordered, "You have thirty seconds to get out of my store or I'm going to have you arrested for trespassing and disturbing the peace."

"And I'll have him charged with assault." The idiot had pulled a backbone out of somewhere. Hope really wished he hadn't bothered, because it was only going to get him hurt worse.

Sighing, Hope leaned against the doorway and crossed her arms over her chest. "Good luck with that. Sheriff Grant is my godfather. Gage is a town hero. Do you really think they're going to arrest him? Especially when Lexi and I tell them that you swung first."

"He doesn't have a mark on him."

"That can be remedied," Gage promised ominously.

"Oh, and if one word of this—" Hope waved her hand around the kitchen "—finds its way into print, Lexi will be filing charges of stalking, professional misconduct and sexual harassment."

"And I'll tack on a suit for libel against you and anyone who runs the story."

Hope knew that wouldn't stick, and if Brandon was any kind of reporter he would, too. But she had a feeling the *Courier* wouldn't appreciate that kind of publicity. And she knew even the whiff of misconduct could ruin the man's career.

He spluttered, snapped his mouth shut and glared at them. Hope grinned evilly. Apparently, Brandon knew that, too. Maybe he wasn't as stupid as she'd feared.

The second the front door chimed his disappearance, Lexi crumbled. Bravado and anger had been holding her together and now that Brandon was gone...

Angry tears streamed down her face. She pushed against her brother's hold on her, but Gage didn't put her down. Instead, he shifted her in his arms, cradled her against his chest and walked across the room to a chair.

How could a man as big and broad as Gage Harper be so gentle? Hope had never seen this side of him, although she shouldn't have been surprised. He'd always been protective of the people he cared about—especially Lexi.

"Don't," he whispered into the crown of her hair. "He isn't worth it."

"You don't think I know that?" she lamented through her tears. "But that doesn't stop it from hurting. I thought he liked *me*. All he wanted was dirt on you."

Realizing she needed to give them some privacy, Hope walked into the front room, flipped the sign to Closed and headed Sheriff Grant off at the pass.

12

EVERYONE AROUND HIM KEPT getting hurt. Tanner. Lexi. Because of him.

The look on his sister's face had crushed him.

Gage paced restlessly around his childhood bedroom, searching for something that would make the churning sensation in his belly stop. Nothing did.

Where was a plane when you needed one to jump out of?

Growling in frustration, Gage spun to head out on the Harley—as close as he was going to get to an adrenaline rush in Sweetheart. But the sight of Hope standing in the doorway stopped him.

The door was closed behind her, one shoulder pressed against the jamb. How long had she been there?

Her arms were crossed beneath her breasts, pushing them against the tight curve of the jacket she'd worn this morning. From a prone spot on her bed he'd watched her put it on.

What really bothered him was that he hadn't even heard her come in. God, what was wrong with him? A few weeks ago that kind of lapse in awareness could have cost lives—his or someone else's. That made the agitation jangling through him worse.

The idea of losing his edge did not sit well.

"How did you know?" he asked, warily. It was a question that had been plaguing him for hours.

She ignored his question. "I came to see how you're doing. I've already been by Lexi's."

And that wasn't going to work for him. "How did you know?"

She glanced away, her gaze darting around the room. "Let's just say I received an anonymous tip."

The fact that she couldn't look him in the eye said differently. "Anonymous my ass. Who was it?"

Tiny lines crinkled the space across the bridge of her nose. Gage wanted to step up to her, press a kiss there and smooth out the evidence of her upset. Why? What was wrong with him that even as he realized she was keeping something from him, his instinct was to say it didn't matter?

It did. So he stayed right where he was.

Finally, she looked at him, serious and solemn. "I'm not going to tell you, Gage, so you might as well drop it. It doesn't matter."

Something in the set of her mouth made him think otherwise, but short of employing some of the torture tactics he'd gotten firsthand knowledge of, he couldn't make her tell him.

"No question, Brandon's a self-serving jerk, but don't think that excuses what you did, Gage."

He sucked in a deep breath and wished it hadn't been full of that spicy and decadent scent that was solely hers.

He pressed both hands against the door behind her and leaned closer, anyway.

"The only thing I did was defend my sister's honor. And I'd do the exact same thing again if I had to."

A single, red-tipped fingernail flicked down his nose. "I know. And give him a sensational story. Before all he had was secondary information from your sister about your childhood. Easy to find most of it without getting her involved. What Brandon wanted, and couldn't get because Lexi didn't know, was a firsthand account of your capture and rescue. What you gave him was even more than he expected—scandal."

"How do you know that?"

"Because I run a newspaper. It's the story we want to publish."

"The story I won't give you."

She nodded, slowly.

"What was I supposed to do?"

Sadness clouded Hope's green-gold eyes. "Stop for thirty seconds and take a deep breath before leaping off into the abyss. Something you've never been real good at." Her voice was full of resignation and disappointment.

He hated that just as much as the pain on Lexi's face. Wanting to wipe the expression away, he did the only thing guaranteed to accomplish the goal. He leaned down and kissed her, filling the connection with all the churning restlessness and energy that filled him.

He half expected her to reject him, had been waiting for the moment when the past met the present and she crushed him yet again, but it didn't happen.

She gave in to the pressure, meeting him with enough roiling passion to make him forget anything. Forget everything. He knew he shouldn't use her to anesthetize himself, but she felt so good.

When he moved to pull the jacket from her shoulders, her soft hands stopped him.

Her eyes were hot and her breath hitched as she said, "Your parents are downstairs."

Like he cared. He wanted her. She wanted him. They were both adults. Besides... Pressing his hips tight against hers, he settled the swollen length of his erection right where he knew it would do the most damage. And then rocked against her over and over again, torturing them both in the sweetest way.

"Do you have any idea how many times I fantasized about you in this room? How many times I woke up hard as a rock from an X-rated dream that starred your hands and mouth all over me?"

Her pupils dilated, her eyes straying over his shoulder. He didn't have to follow her gaze to know she was looking at the bed. His bed.

He'd had her in her bed, floor, kitchen, shower, but in that moment none of those was enough. He wanted her right now, right here. Where he'd always dreamed of having her.

Leaning closer, he ran his lips over the sensitive curve of her ear. And whispered, "I don't know how many times I touched myself, thinking of you."

Gage found the warm spot right behind her ear and sucked. She gasped softly and shuddered, her eyelids weighting with the same desire that filled him.

He tasted her skin, running kisses down the side of her throat. "Only you."

Without asking for permission, Gage swept her legs out from under her and carried her over to his bed. It

was smaller than hers, only a double, but as long as she was in it that was all he needed.

He should have known Hope had never been one to accept things at face value. She pushed. She questioned. He hated and loved that about her.

Her back had barely hit the mattress before she was bounding up to grab him and pull him down beside her. "Fantasies, huh? What kind of fantasies?"

Tucking her beneath him, Gage rolled until they were stretched diagonally across the bed. "Well, there was one with you, me and Spider-Man."

"Kinky."

"But I was ten and it was hardly explicit so I don't think that counts."

"There go my plans for using that sticky web."

Gage grinned down at her. She was so beautiful that it hurt. If someone had told him a month ago he'd be holding Hope Rawlings in his bed he'd have laughed and called the man a liar.

How quickly things could change.

How bizarre life could be.

But he refused to let the whys ruin this moment together.

Resolved, he rolled his hips against her, pressing her into the mattress. She arched her back, meeting him, a smile tugging at her lips.

"Anything else? Maybe something I could fulfill for you?"

A long-dead fantasy flashed across his mind, past and present melding together. How many times had he woken up hard and throbbing from a dream of her sucking him off? Only this time when the vision popped into his mind it wasn't the teenaged Hope with her long tawny hair and serious green eyes, it was this Hope. The sexy, contained, delightfully challenging woman she'd become.

"Well..." he drawled, letting the full weight of his Southern accent pull at the vowel.

Her hands found the edge of his shirt and the strip of skin where it had ridden up his ribs. The teasing point of her fingernails raked across his abs, making the muscles jump.

"Yes?" she asked, her sultry eyes flashing with interest.

He touched her lips. The bottom one contorted when he dragged a fingertip against it. Her mouth parted and she sucked the single digit into the hot recesses.

The tantalizing edge of her tongue scraped against the sensitive pad of his finger. It was as if she had a direct path to his cock. A jagged bolt of electricity shot through him, turning him rock-hard.

Gage groaned, dropping his head back at the feel of her.

"Kiss me," he ordered, pulling his finger from her mouth.

She melded their mouths together and brought him low. As devastating as the kiss was, it wasn't what he wanted.

"That's not what I meant," he said breathlessly when she finally let him go.

Her gaze glittered with impish delight. "I know."

The air backed up into his lungs. With steady pressure, she pushed against his shoulders until he dropped back onto the bed. She rose above him. The soft strands of her hair fell around her face, blocking out everything but the vision of her.

He scraped her hair back, anchoring it at the nape of her neck. He wanted to see her.

That grin only grew when she dipped down his body and opened his jeans. Her hands were cool and steady. Or maybe that was just because he was shaking and on fire.

She found him, hard and throbbing with a need only she could stir inside him. She stroked him once, not nearly enough, before she paused to strip him of his clothes. She didn't stop with his jeans and shorts, insisting that he lose everything. When he realized he couldn't sway her determination, he quickly complied.

Although the moment he was stretched out in front of her, completely naked, while she still had every stitch of clothing on, he thought maybe that had been a tactical error. It felt wrong. He wanted to see her. Touch all of her.

But when he moved to return the favor she'd waved a single finger in his face and said, "Uh, uh, uh," while moving out of the range of his searching hands.

Her hands ran roughly across his chest and abs, heading exactly where he wanted. But she didn't touch him. His traitorous cock leaped, anyway, absolutely certain it was about to get what it wanted.

"Not yet," she murmured. Instead, she let her hands continue down the flexed ridge of his thighs.

She leaned forward. The ends of her hair tickled over his abs. Her hot breath wafted across his erection. It wasn't enough. He thrust his hips forward, trying to reach what he wanted.

She just smirked, pulling back to kneel between his spread thighs. Slowly, she ran her hands up her own body. Her fingers lingered over her own breasts and his eyes zeroed in on the tenting peaks of her nipples against the tight cotton of her shirt.

Hope pressed a thumb against one of them, rolling it beneath the pressure. Her eyelids slid closed and she dropped her head back with pleasure.

Gage shifted, wanted to be the one to touch her. But the moment he moved her eyes popped open and speared him. A single eyebrow rose in a pointed order. He debated the merits of doing what she wanted and finally decided to settle back.

The reward was her taking her shirt and bra off, at least letting his eyes touch her if nothing else could.

She teased him and delighted in it, using the flat of her tongue to lick him like the best ice cream cone. She stroked up and down, the moist heat of her breath bathing over him.

Finally, her bright pink lips parted, taking him deep inside. His entire body tensed for the unbelievable reality and the remarkable fantasy to finally merge.

He wasn't disappointed. Actually, he was blown away, because there was no comparison.

She sucked hard, slowly letting him slip through the pressurized tunnel of her mouth. Her tongue stroked him. Damn, she felt so good.

He was close, and until the moment when that band of pressure built at the center of his back, ready to let go, he'd thought he wanted to come with her face buried in his lap. But as good as it felt, it wasn't enough.

He wanted to look in her eyes when he came. He wanted to know she was right there with him, sharing the moment in every possible way.

Finding a strength he hadn't known he possessed, Gage grasped her by the shoulders, tore her away from his erection and had her flat on her back in less than ten seconds.

Hope blinked up at him, her mouth puckered open, disoriented. The expression was cute. He rather liked to fluster her because it happened so rarely. Efficient, structured, determined Hope.

Gage tore at the few clothes that she'd kept on, making quick work of them. At the same time he managed to find a condom from the bedside drawer, spent about a nanosecond worrying how old it could be before deciding he really didn't care and rolled the sucker over his aching erection.

The scent of her arousal—warm, spicy—slammed into him. It was more temptation than he could deny. He spread the folds of her sex to find her slippery with wanting him. Apparently, her little teasing job hadn't only worked on him.

He slowly sank home, devastated by the perfect feel of her. She made a quiet gasp and arched up to meet him. Her swollen sex tightened around him, pulling him closer. He paused, relishing the way they came together. A perfect fit.

Her body stretched, welcoming him even as he slowly, deliberately moved against her. Her feet scraped restlessly against the bed. He buried his forehead against her throat, breathing her in and letting everything about her wrap around him. Her hips writhed, searching for more.

Gage pulled out and quickly thrust back in. Her eyes widened and glazed. Sharp teeth bit into her bottom lip. Running the pad of his finger over it, he freed it and leaned down to suck it into his own mouth.

They worked together, finding a rhythm that rang

the most pleasure out of each and every joining. Hope began to whimper...soft, urgent sounds that drove him to give her more.

Nails raked down his back, taking skin and leaving marks. He didn't care, but he understood her need for something to hold on to. The storm building inside him was almost more than he could bear.

At least alone.

It was more than physical. More than sex. Reaching behind him, he grabbed her hands, threaded their fingers together and pressed them into the mattress beside her head. Held tight to her.

Unable to tear his gaze away from her, he watched. And knew the moment the pressure building inside her snapped. Ecstasy flooded through her, spilling out and crashing over him.

Her release rocked through him just as surely as his own. Stars burst across his vision, blinding him to everything but Hope. His entire world narrowed down to her.

When had that happened? When had she become everything?

HOPE WATCHED HIM THROUGH heavy-lidded eyes. His hair was damp from the shower they'd just shared. Thank heaven his parents' room was downstairs because they hadn't exactly been quiet and she was embarrassed enough as it was.

Gage grasped the ends of the towel he'd draped across his shoulders after drying his head. She'd been so preoccupied before that she hadn't really stopped to look at his thumbs now that they were unbandaged.

Her stomach flip-flopped sickly. She'd never been

one to be bothered by blood, but the physical reminder of what he'd been through… It was hard to look at.

He followed her gaze, glancing down at his fisted hands and then back at her.

"You can't let it go, can you?"

Slowly, Hope reached for him. She wrapped a hand around the sharp edge of his hip and pulled him closer. Stiffly, he let her tug him to the bed. His knees hit the mattress, but he didn't fall beside her.

Hope grasped one hand and, one by one, uncurled his fingers until he let the towel swing free. She squeezed, stretched out his thumb.

"It bothers me."

Gage tried to pull his hand out of her hold. "I'm sorry. I'll cover them up."

Her forehead crinkled with annoyance. "That's not what I meant. It bothers me to think about you in pain." She placed the barest kiss right above the exposed nail bed. "It must have hurt."

Gage shrugged. "It wasn't pleasant."

A strangled laugh lodged inside her chest, aching just a little, as if she'd swallowed something hard and couldn't quite get it down. There was nothing funny about this. "Somehow I think that's an understatement."

He didn't answer her, just stood there in silence and let her stroke his hand.

"Tell me."

She expected him to refuse, to pull away from her and shut her out like he did everyone else. So she was shocked when he didn't.

"They took pliers and applied pressure to my thumbs until the nails cracked. Then they ripped the pieces out."

"Holy hell."

"There was nothing holy about it."

"No," she choked out, "there wasn't."

She'd known whatever happened hadn't been good. It didn't take a genius to figure out. And hearing the specifics was gut-churning enough. But what bothered her most was the even, steady voice he'd delivered them with.

Like he was issuing a grocery list instead of talking about torture.

"What did they want?" she forced herself to ask. Not because she wanted to know, but because she knew that he needed to talk about this to someone. If that someone was her…she'd find a way to get through it.

When her mother died, Gage had been there for her. A ten-year-old boy who'd never dealt with loss himself had been one of the only people to understand. To sit there in silence with her when she couldn't talk about it, or listen to her endless stream of words when she couldn't hold them inside anymore.

"Information. Details about our plans, our troops, our informants, whatever I could give them."

"You didn't give them anything." It wasn't a question because Hope already knew the answer.

Her eyes strayed to the thumb she still held. Could she have lasted through that kind of deliberately inflicted pain? No, she didn't think so. She wasn't strong enough.

"I would have crumbled."

"No, you wouldn't have."

Hope made a sound of disagreement.

"You forget, I've seen your determination in action. Nothing sways you once you make up your mind about something."

Not exactly true. Where had her dedication been when she needed to resist him?

Twelve years ago she'd been so angry with him. And scared. Scared to let herself love him and lose him. Scared of the danger he was willingly walking into and his need to push the boundaries and test everyone—including himself.

She hadn't even lasted two days before she'd given in and let him touch her. If he'd stayed around back then would she have been able to resist longer? Or would her anger have dissolved and left her open and vulnerable just like now?

"When there are lives at stake you find the strength. Anything I'd told them would have been used to harm American soldiers. I was already responsible for our capture, I wouldn't add that to my conscience."

"You were willing to die." Again, not a question. The nature of his job involved a willingness to make that sacrifice if that's what was needed.

That reality scared the shit out of her. It hurt, deep inside. The pain of loss was recognizable even though it had been so many years since she'd felt it. Not that time really mattered when you were talking about that kind of grief.

Losing her mother, losing Gage, would have hurt the same. Even before she'd dropped her defenses and let him in.

"To protect my brothers? To exchange my life for the thousands of men and woman who served with me? You bet."

Knowing he'd make that choice and hearing him voice it were two different things. What made it more difficult was that it went beyond that. "To protect one," she whispered. Because that was really the rub. Choosing to protect lots of people was just noble. And easy. The greater good. Choosing to sacrifice yourself for one single person…that took guts, commitment and a willful recklessness.

The kind of recklessness that sent a chill down her spine. That made her want to wrap her arms around herself and curl into a ball. Because, while she admired him for that courage and integrity, she realized making that sacrifice was the easy part.

Learning to live without him—and with the guilt of wishing he could make a different choice—would be hard for those he left behind.

He didn't answer her because they both knew what she'd said was true.

But something he'd said earlier finally registered. "What do you mean you were responsible for what happened? How could you possibly be responsible?"

13

GAGE CLOSED HIS EYES. He'd been hoping she wouldn't pick up on the detail he'd let slip. He should have known better. Hope liked things neat and tidy.

He opened his eyes again and looked into her upturned face. She watched him, her green-gold eyes patiently waiting.

Cupping her face, he ran the pad of his finger across her soft skin. He wanted to tell her. The urge surprised him. How could that be possible?

Even as he tried to issue a stern order to his mouth to stay shut, the words were falling out.

"I screwed up and got us captured."

He didn't want to look at her, to see the horror and disappointment on her face, so he dropped down onto the bed beside her, giving her his back.

Behind him, her weight shifted. Part of him expected her to just get up and walk away. And, really, he wouldn't have blamed her. But she didn't.

The sharp jab of her knees pressed against his hips. Her hands brushed lightly across his shoulders, down his arms and up his back. Finally, she wrapped herself around him from behind and rested her chin against his back.

Beneath her touch he was rigid. Every muscle in his body was pulled tight with the memories and regret he'd been fighting for weeks.

She didn't ask him to continue, which is probably why he did.

"I was...restless that day. I'd just found out a good friend had died. Senselessly, in an accident, which actually made it worse. I was pissed and upset."

"Understandable."

"Maybe, but I didn't deal with it well. Instead of taking a day or two to clear my head like I should have, I went in and asked to be sent out on assignment."

"A distraction. A way to push your body so your mind could rest."

Gage nodded. "Exactly." It should have helped that she understood. It didn't. It just reinforced the feeling that he was entirely too predictable. A woman he hadn't seen for twelve years knew exactly what he'd been looking for when at the time he hadn't had a clue. What did that say about him?

Certainly nothing good.

"Boy, did I get it. Our assignment was simply to visit a local village and to gather any intel our regular contacts had to report. Simple."

Hope rubbed her cheek against his back. "Famous last words."

And they almost were. They were so damn lucky no one had died. That was probably the only thing that let him sleep at night.

"One of the kids was acting funny. A boy, twelve or

thirteen, that I'd talked to before. He was jumpy. That should have been my first clue something was wrong, but I thought it was because he was scared about sharing the information he had in such a public place. When he beckoned us to follow him, I did."

He could see the men, the kid, the place so clearly he could have been standing there. A bitter scent greeted them when they crossed the low threshold into a house. Darkened hallways.

"The house was sprawling, probably big enough to shelter a huge extended family. The inside rooms had no windows. It was so dark, even in the middle of the day."

And like the inside of a maze, one room opening up to a hallway with a handful more, and on and on.

"Within a few turns we were lost. Each room looked exactly like the next. The team swept the house as we went, but it was so big and they'd been waiting for us...."

"It was a trap."

"Yeah."

"So how was that your fault?"

Slowly, Gage turned his head and looked straight into her eyes. "Because we shouldn't have gone in. That sixth sense you develop out on the battlefield, the one that keeps your ass safe, told me something was wrong, but I ignored it."

She stared back at him, steadily.

"I ignored it *and* protocol. The house hadn't been cleared, but I didn't want to let the boy get away. I knew if we didn't follow him whatever intel he had would be gone. I pushed, like I always do. But this time I wasn't the only one to pay the price."

He dropped his gaze to Hope's mouth. It would be

so easy to drown himself in the taste of her. To use sex and her presence to push away everything he wanted to forget.

But he'd never been a coward and he wasn't starting today.

So instead, he pulled his gaze back up to hers and waited for the recriminations he knew he deserved.

"No one died, Gage."

"Maybe not, but they could have."

"Didn't."

"My friend lost his leg."

"And you were tortured. I'm not saying there aren't scars, I'm saying the wounds aren't fatal. For anyone. You made a mistake. It happens. Despite what you'd like everyone to believe. you are human."

He laughed, the sound bedraggled and drowning in despair. What she said might be true, but it didn't help. "I'm supposed to be more than human, Hope. A Ranger. The best of the best. The strongest of the strong."

Hope pressed a kiss to the back of his neck. The tiny hairs there stood at attention, immediately responding in an unnerving approximation of that warning itch he'd ignored.

The last thing he'd expected was a kiss. It was the last thing he deserved.

"The question is, what are you going to do about it?"

"What do you mean? What *can* I do about it? It's over."

"Maybe. But I'm talking more about you. Are you going to take chunks out of your own hide every day for the rest of your life in penance? Are you going to wallow in self-disgust? Or are you going to figure out how to move past this? The way I see it you have two choices, let it destroy you or do something about it."

Ever the pragmatist, that was his Hope. He should have known she'd cut through all the bullshit and tell him the truth. At least she hadn't tried to convince him he hadn't done anything wrong as Tanner had done.

She had a point. A good one. In this state he wasn't good for anything or anyone. He definitely wouldn't trust himself in a combat situation, and though he wasn't ready to admit it to anyone else, he wasn't sure he'd ever trust himself there again.

He'd been trained to rely on his instincts to protect himself and the men around him. He no longer trusted those instincts. He was pretty screwed up at the moment, and this was one time he knew better than to push himself. It wouldn't be fair to the other men in his unit that depended on him to have their back.

One thing was for sure, he wouldn't go back if he couldn't completely trust himself to protect the brothers with whom he served.

But that was a bridge he didn't have to cross. At least not yet.

What bothered him was that even if Hope made sense, her advice was easy to offer and damn hard to follow. Exactly how was he supposed to move past the guilt?

Rather than ask her, and get an answer he wasn't ready to deal with, he settled on the next best thing. Kissing, touching and holding her. When she was with him, at least some of the turmoil he'd been carting around inside him eased.

Including the stuff that had always been there. Restless energy. That need for challenge and danger. When she was there, those needs weren't.

Bridging the gap between them, Gage pressed his mouth to hers. Her hands slipped up his chest. She leaned into the kiss and asked for more.

Desire overwhelmed him. It was heady and delicious. So much more pleasurable than the things he was trying to forget.

DAMN. SHE'D FALLEN IN LOVE with him. What was she supposed to do with that? How had she let this happen?

Hope stared down at him. His mouth, hands and body were more relaxed than she'd seen since he'd been home. The skin under his eyes only carried the faintest hint of the bruise he'd gotten at the fight.

Man, he was a fast healer.

How could she have given him her heart just as quickly?

Or maybe she'd always been on the verge of doing that. If that was the case she'd picked a hell of a time to give in.

Helpless tears burned her eyes. Hope angrily pushed them away. They wouldn't help.

There were so many reasons why this wouldn't work. The most important one being that he would hurt her. He might not mean to but…

Her mom had been ripped from her. The way of it, so sudden, had hurt almost as much as the gaping hole in her life. A car accident on an icy winter road driving home from work in Charleston. There one minute and gone the next.

Her dad had tried to fill the gap, but a girl needed her mother. Especially during those teenage years when she tried to figure out what kind of woman she was going to be. What kind of wife and mother. She'd lost the example just when she'd needed it most.

She could lose Gage the same way. Boom! In one second he'd be gone and she'd be alone and devastated. Without him there to help her through the agony.

He was a fighter and had been long before becoming a soldier. The same things that made him a great soldier—that damn reckless streak, honor, bravery, determination—made him a terrible bet to build your life on.

Hope's gaze was drawn to the uncovered wounds where his thumbnails should have been. One of these days he was going to end up dead.

A bomb, a gun, a fight or faulty parachute…. One risk too many. It didn't matter when or how. What mattered was that it would happen. Today, tomorrow, ten years from now.

Even thinking about it had her chest tightening so much she couldn't breathe.

She couldn't do this. She couldn't stay here.

GAGE WOKE ALONE. And wasn't happy about it. What was worse was that the bed beside him was stone cold, telling him that Hope had left a long time ago.

Why had she skulked out in the middle of the night like a common thief? They were going to have to discuss this.

He tried not to let it bother him that he'd opened up to her, shared not only the worst experience of his life, but also his role in what had happened and the guilt that went right along with it, and she'd disappeared in the night.

Dread and a sense of foreboding rolled through him.

It was the same sixth sense that had kept him safe more times than he could count.

This wasn't good. Climbing out of bed, Gage headed for the shower.

He'd been so caught up in everything that he hadn't realized what day it was until he walked into the kitchen to find his parents standing in the center kissing. A vase full of roses—ten red and two white—sat in the middle of the table. It was the same predictably sweet bouquet his dad had gotten for his mom every Valentine's Day for as long as he could remember. The red were for their love, the white for each of their children.

"Happy Valentine's Day." His mama beamed at him over his dad's shoulder. Her eyes glowed with happiness. He wanted that. To love and be loved thirty years later.

He wanted that with Hope.

The thought surprised him. But it shouldn't have. He'd loved her for as long as he could remember. His mind was spinning as he stood silently and stared at his parents.

His mom's smile faltered. She glanced worriedly up at his dad and then back at him. "Is Hope coming down?"

That jerked Gage out of his stupor.

"Oh, don't look so guilty, Gage. You're an adult. Besides, we like Hope and always have. She's welcome to stay anytime."

Well. Okay. It wasn't that he'd expected to keep Hope's visit a secret. Or that his parents would kick up a fuss. It was more that he'd expected all of them to just pretend it hadn't happened. Sort of like don't ask, don't tell.

His dad swung slowly around to face him, his arm still wrapped tightly around his mom's waist.

"I have to admit I was worried when Edith told me Hope had bought you for the week, what with your history. I never did understand what happened between you before you left, but I knew it wasn't good. By the time I'd learned of it, though, there was nothing I could do. The couples had already been announced."

Hope had paid to be coupled with him? Why would she do that? Thinking back to that night, when the announcement had been made, he realized she hadn't looked surprised. Nervous, yes. Wary, absolutely. Shocked, no.

"Why would she do that?"

"Isn't it obvious?" His mom asked. "She had a change of heart and wanted the chance to fix what happened before you left."

Gage rolled that notion around inside his head, rejecting it almost as quickly as his mom had offered it. Hope had definitely not been repentant for rejecting him. In fact, not once had she mentioned it or even apologized for it, not that he needed or wanted her to.

But if she'd bought time with him for that purpose wouldn't that have been the logical place to start? And if Hope was anything, it was logical. Hell, she probably would have made a list.

As far as he could see, there was no list.

In fact, at first she'd been rather reluctant to even be next to him. He'd had to practically drag her out onto the dance floor at the cocktail party. And she hadn't loosened up, not really, until the next afternoon in the rain outside the bowling alley.

Sure she'd begrudgingly offered him comfort when

he crashed her place in the middle of the night. And at the fight she'd asked about Afghani— His thought trailed off.

She'd asked him about Afghanistan. Not once but at least twice. And she'd slept with him. Sure, she'd chased reporters off her front lawn with a shotgun, but that could just as easily have been a stunt to claim her territory rather than to defend him.

With a groan, Gage sank into one of the kitchen chairs and dropped his head into his hands.

"Honey, are you okay?" his mom asked, alarm turning her voice shrill.

And he'd told Hope everything she'd wanted to know. And more. Last night.

Rage blasted through him. His mama laid a hand on his bent back. With a roar, he surged to his feet, knocking it off.

She'd slept with him and he'd spilled his guts.

How stupid could one man get?

_14_

HOPE STARED AT THE CURSOR on the blank document she'd just opened. Great. The first piece she'd taken in weeks and she couldn't write a damn thing. Her brain was empty. Empty of everything but what Gage had told her and the fear that came with it—for him and for herself.

No, she had no intention of using the information he'd given her. After the Brandon incident the last place she wanted to work was the _Courier_. But she was a writer, even if she didn't get to use the skills as often as she liked, and part of her itched to put the details down so she could process them for herself.

How else was she supposed to deal with the horror and pain and guilt he'd shared with her? Just the thought of him being beaten and tortured…he was dealing with it a hell of a lot better than she would be.

If that had been her, she'd have been a quivering pile of fear.

Gage was so damn strong. Too strong for his own good.

With a sigh of frustration, Hope finally gave in,

knowing she wouldn't get any actual work done until she'd spit her emotions out onto the page.

Everything faded away as her world coalesced to nothing but the white rectangle on her screen and the black words racing across it. She set down details—some in his words and some in her own. But mostly Hope wrote about how much she admired him for protecting the men he was responsible for. The look in his eyes as he'd poured everything out to her. How strong and honorable and broken he was.

Pretty soon the ramblings turned into what she could do to help him. It was an agenda for herself that ended with two bold words—love him.

They scared her so she erased them.

And just in time because Gage stormed into her office, slamming her door closed behind him.

Fury blazed from his eyes. She'd expected him to be a little miffed when he woke and she was gone, but really, this was too much.

"Why did you leave?" he asked, his voice deep and dark.

She'd been prepared for the question, although she had to admit that his jarring entrance had set her off her game. Still, she trotted out the bluff she'd prepared, anyway. "Because I didn't feel right sleeping beneath your parents' roof."

"Bullshit."

Hope's heart stuttered in her chest. His golden eyes narrowed, zeroing straight on her. She couldn't help but feel open and vulnerable. Could he see just how much she cared about him? Would he use it against her?

How was she going to extricate her heart from this fix without losing pieces of herself?

"You got what you wanted last night and decided it wasn't worth sticking around anymore."

Hope opened her mouth to issue another argument, but had to shut it again when his words sank in and she realized she had no idea what he was talking about.

"Excuse me?"

"Last night. The minute I told you about Afghanistan you disappeared."

She felt sick.

"My leaving had nothing to do with what you told me."

Which technically wasn't true. What he'd told her had everything to do with why she'd left, but not the way he obviously thought.

His jaw flexed. He took a menacing step toward her and growled, "Liar. There's guilt all over your face. Trust me, I'm intimate with the emotion and recognize it when I see it."

Hope's first reaction was to crumble beneath the weight of his anger. It would have been easy to do. But that wasn't who she was. She refused to let him have that kind of hold over her. It was exactly what she'd always been afraid of, that she would lose herself to him and then lose *him*.

"You're right. I do feel guilty, but not for the reason you seem to think. Everything you told me last night…" The helplessness she'd felt looking down at him, knowing that he could never change and if she really loved him she wouldn't want him to, resurfaced. "It scared the crap out of me, Gage."

Hope sent the chair at her knees rolling backward. The added space gave her room to walk away. Slipping around the desk, she placed it between them and felt stronger with the barrier there. Safer. Not from him, but from herself.

"Why do you think I never tried to take our friendship further when we were younger?"

"Because you weren't interested."

"Wrong. I was interested. Very interested. Did you never wonder why I didn't date anyone else?"

His teeth clipped off a single word. "No."

"I didn't want to date anyone else. No guy could measure up to you. That damn sparkle in your eyes. The charming way your mouth curls higher on one side when you smile. Really smile. The relentless way you attack life. Your mischievousness. Or the way you stood up against your father and refused to do what he wanted. Strength and integrity, they went bone-deep with you even back then."

Confusion crossed his face, crowding out the hard expression. Slowly, he sank into the chair she'd just abandoned. "Then why did you say no?"

"Because right along with that determination came a breakneck need for something more. You were searching—for acceptance, understanding, I have no idea what. The problem was you always pushed—yourself, your friends, your parents, me. You weren't content to throw yourself into the abyss, you wanted company.

"I had plans, Gage. Dreams of my own, and I couldn't take the risk that letting you in would mean I'd lose that for myself. Lose my own strength because it couldn't compare to yours."

He swallowed. The long column of his tanned throat worked tantalizingly, drawing her gaze and distracting her. That was exactly what she was talking about!

Just being in the same room with him had the ability to make everything else unimportant.

If he touched her right now she'd be powerless to stop him from doing whatever he wanted—and damn the fact that she was in her office, in the middle of the day, behind schedule on a new story that needed to go to press.

"And then you joined the army. Probably the most perfect job for you. Every day pushing you physically, challenging you and filled with danger. And I knew eventually you'd push too far and end up dead."

To protect herself, Hope dropped her gaze from his to the top of her immaculate desk. It didn't help. She still knew he was there and wanted desperately to say, "The hell with everything else," and just give in to what she wanted. Him.

But she couldn't do that. Not when cold sweat popped out across her brow at the mere thought of throwing caution to the wind and telling him that she loved him and wanted him in her life.

Between the two of them, Gage was the caution-throwing one.

A strangled sound from deep in his throat had Hope jerking her gaze back to his.

He didn't have to say a single word. She knew from the expression on his face and the direction of his eyes exactly what he was looking at. The document she'd been writing. About everything he'd told her last night.

She protested, "That isn't what you think." The words were guttural and jumbled up as she tried to push them out faster than her lips and tongue could move.

With deliberation, he reached for the mouse on her desk and with his newly bandaged thumb rolled the little wheel in the center. She tried to snatch it from his grasp, but he just picked it up and moved it out of her reach. Damn wireless technology.

"That isn't for the paper, Gage. I swear."

His skin turned red before blanching white. "Funny. It's on your work computer at the paper. It reads like a feature article."

After several tense moments, Gage hung his head. His hands spread wide across the gleaming surface of her desk. Carefully, he stood. The wood groaned as he pushed against it.

Silence strangled her. The pressure of it was a living thing, squeezing the life right out of her. "Look at me," she whispered, deeply afraid of what she might see.

And she had every right to be.

Gradually, Gage lifted his head and looked at her with eyes so blank they could have been dead. But they weren't. They were so much worse.

Uncaring. Unfeeling. Indifferent.

How was that possible?

"You know what? Publish your article, Hope. You deserve it. You worked harder for it than anyone else. I was offered a heck of a lot of money from all sorts of news agencies and talk shows. But none of them offered to sleep with me. You had the perfect trump card, didn't you? Something you always knew I wanted and no one else could give. That kind of commitment should be rewarded."

His words were a punch straight to the gut. She couldn't breathe. Her lungs heaved. Her mouth worked, but nothing flowed into her body. The world went black and bright lights popped across the desolate space.

Somehow she made it over to one of the chairs in

front of her desk. She had no idea how long she sat there, staring blankly into space. But when she finally blinked back to reality she was alone.

Outside the open door the familiar sounds of a working newspaper greeted her. A telephone. Someone typing on a keyboard. Murmured voices.

They weren't enough.

When had they stopped being enough?

A SOFT RAIN PATTERED down onto the visor covering his face. He'd thrown on a helmet, the rain and Hope's admonishing voice thick in his ear. He couldn't even get away from her here.

In retaliation—and to show that she didn't matter—Gage pushed the bike faster. He raced down Main and elicited evil glances from several of the people inside the shops.

Finally! Things were returning to normal. Maybe now everyone would stop walking on eggshells around him and treat him like regular Gage Harper, disappointing mayor's son and boy who let the goats loose in the high school, instead of some exalted war hero.

He didn't want the title. Didn't deserve it.

The devil inside him urged him to just let go. To forget everything. Afghanistan. Tanner. Micah. Hope.

As he twisted the throttle, the bike roared beneath him. Gage drove faster. The pavement was slick and it required all of his attention to keep the growling Harley on the road, which was a good thing because then he didn't have to think about what he'd left behind.

Although, the plan didn't work very well. Images of Hope still managed to creep in. Her eyes spitting fire at him the night of the cocktail party. Wet and bedraggled outside the bowling alley. Staring up at him through hot, passion-filled eyes as he drove deep inside her. The way she laughed and argued and *knew* him.

Dammit! How was he supposed to just let her go? To believe that she'd faked everything—okay, not *everything*—to get what she wanted?

Even knowing what she'd done—manipulating him for her own ends—he didn't want to let her go. She was the best thing that had happened to him in a very long time. Possibly ever.

He couldn't believe that she'd done it just for the story. Maybe he was naive, but everything inside him said there was more. That she really cared about him and always had. The words that she'd said first, her reasons for rejecting him when they were younger, rang in his ears. And they rang true.

When he was with her the doubts he'd been having no longer mattered. The restlessness he'd always fought against disappeared. He was steadier. On firmer ground.

He saw the possibilities. His life was dangerous and transient. He went where he was needed for as long as necessary. And in the past twelve years he hadn't worried about what he was leaving behind. Not once.

He did now. With her he wanted more than just a good time and a warm goodbye. And always had.

Gage was a fighter. That's what he did. It's what he was good at. So why was he willing to just turn tail and run away from this? From her?

He'd fought for his life. For the lives of the men he was responsible for. He'd looked dangerous, ruthless and sadistic men in the face and laughed at their attempts to break him.

The reality was they couldn't because nothing they'd

done to him had mattered. The physical pain he could survive.

The thought of losing Hope sent him into a mental tailspin. Now that his anger was spent, he had nothing to keep the throbbing ache of her betrayal at bay.

It rushed him, blinding him for several seconds.

The loss of concentration and winding, slippery roads made a terrible combination. One moment the bike was racing across open road. The next he was spinning out of control.

He and the Harley hurtled through the air, the tires squealing uselessly as they tried to grab on to asphalt. He headed off the road at an odd angle, bumping across grass and gravel and heading straight for a grove of trees thirty yards away.

Not good.

Metal and wood connected with a terrible crunching sound. Jagged pain tore through his leg, stealing his breath. His shoulder connected with something hard. He heard a bone snap. He was coherent enough to wonder why it didn't hurt.

He and the bike came to rest between two trees. Through the starburst across his visor he could see the brighter color of wood where something—probably metal—had gouged into the bark. A wheel spun drunkenly.

He was still breathing, and conscious. Both good signs.

And then the pain hit. It radiated through him, worse than anything he'd ever felt in his life. It was everywhere.

He had just enough strength to pull the cell phone

out of his jacket pocket. After saying a small prayer of thanks that it still worked, he dialed 911.

And then passed out.

HOPE HAD FINALLY DECIDED to go home. It wasn't as if she was in any frame of mind to work. One of the other writers would have to pick up the piece. It wouldn't be the first time she'd had to reassign something because she didn't have time to write it.

And yet, she still kept trying.

Finally, in the safety of her own home, she'd broken down, crying until she didn't have any more to give.

She'd known he would hurt her.

The problem was, she couldn't completely blame him, could she? Even if she hadn't intended that piece for publication, she had manipulated him with the express intention of getting what she wanted—whether he liked it or not.

Only after he'd left had she realized she hadn't even admitted that. Or told him she was sorry.

Eventually, she'd fallen asleep.

A loud pounding on her front door had her bolting up from the sofa where she'd curled up.

"Huh? What?" she asked no one, spinning confusedly in a circle.

Only when the sound came again did it really register that someone was practically trying to drill through her front door.

Racing over, she yanked it open before her brain kicked in and cautioned her that maybe she should have looked first. Luckily, it was Lexi standing on her stoop and not another horde of reporters.

But it didn't take her long to realize her friend looked

like hell. Her first assumption was that Lexi must still be upset over Brandon. But then she realized her eyes were red-rimmed and swollen with new tears. When she'd left Sugar & Spice yesterday Lexi had been past that stage and well into being pissed. Something else was wrong.

"What?" Hope grabbed onto her friend's arm and hauled her inside.

"Where have you been? I've been calling you for the past hour."

Hope thought back to leaving the office and groaned, realizing she'd been in such a daze that she must have left her cell sitting on her desk. "I walked off and left my phone."

"Of all the days…" Lexi's voice trailed off, thickening with new tears. Hope wrapped her in a hug and offered whatever comfort she could. She had no idea what was going on, but Lexi would tell her soon enough.

Her friend clung to her, mumbling into her hair, "He's been in an accident."

"Who?" Surely Lexi wasn't talking about Brandon. But who else…

In that moment she knew exactly who. All the blood drained from Hope's head, leaving her shaken and pale. Oh, no. Not again. She couldn't go through this again. Her mind flashed to that day so many years ago, when the officer had knocked on the front door and told her dad that her mom was gone.

This time Lexi had come.

Hope's legs refused to hold her up and she collapsed beneath the combined weight of both of them.

"Oh, my God."

A vision of his eerie, calmly irate eyes melded with

him straddling that damn Harley, sunshine washing down over his naked head as he drove away.

It was her fault. This accident was her fault. She should have stopped him. But she'd been so devastated that she hadn't thought. Of course he'd go out and do something reckless and stupid. Like die.

"Oh, my God."

He was dead. It was every nightmare she'd ever had. Absolutely everything she'd been afraid of with Gage come to real life. And she couldn't take it. It hurt too much.

Asshole, she thought desperately. A ragged sob erupted from her. He would survive being captured and tortured to come home and die in a motorcycle accident because he refused to wear a damn helmet.

She was never going to forgive him.

Or herself.

"They're keeping him overnight, but he's been asking for you."

"Wait. What?" Hope shook her head. She had to mentally backpedal, to dovetail what Lexi had just said into the conclusion she'd jumped to. They didn't fit. "He's okay?"

"Well, if you can call twenty stitches in his leg, a collarbone broken in two different places and a hell of a lot of bruises okay, then yeah."

Hope gripped Lexi's shoulders and held her away so she could look into her friend's eyes. "He isn't dead?"

Shock widened Lexi's tear bright eyes. "No! I'm so sorry. I didn't think... I've been holding it together for Mom and Dad. The minute I saw you all the fear and memories and relief just hit me."

"He's alive?" Hope asked again, because she really, really needed to hear the words.

"Yes, he's alive. Banged up. But the doctors said it could have been worse. Luckily he was wearing a helmet."

"He was?" she asked incredulously. "He's never bothered to wear one before. I've been giving him grief about it for days."

"Thank heaven he finally listened to you."

15

HE'D BEEN HIT BY A freight train. Again. Had he been recaptured? He didn't remember returning to Afghanistan, but maybe he'd blocked it. Every muscle, including a few he'd forgotten he had, ached.

His leg throbbed like a son of a bitch and when he tried to roll onto his side he sucked in a sharp breath against the pain that shot across his chest and down his shoulder.

What the hell?

"Lie still." A soft voice floated to him from across the room.

Gage realized his eyes weren't closed. The room was dark. Suddenly a light beside the bed flared on.

Hope stood next to him, watching him with cautious, measured eyes.

And like that everything was fine. Hope was with him and nothing else mattered.

"Do you want me to call the nurse? You can probably have more pain meds."

"No," he croaked through a dry throat. He didn't like the meds. "They make my head fuzzy."

"Brave, stupid man." Reaching over his head, she pressed the big button with the picture of a nurse on it. "Take the medicine. Who cares if you're fuzzy? It isn't like there's anything else for you to do but sleep."

The nurse came in and pushed something into the IV still attached to his arm. He moved to yank it out, but two hands slapped over his, stopping him.

The nurse gave Hope a rueful smile. "You warned me." Transferring her hard gaze to Gage, she threatened, "If you try to pull that IV out I'm going to knock you out completely. Be a good boy." Then she patted him on the cheek.

"I like her," Hope said, crossing her arms over her chest.

"I don't."

"I can't imagine why," she said dryly.

With a resigned sigh, Hope reached behind her and dragged one of the uncomfortable, heavy chairs that were a staple of all hospital rooms over to the side of the bed. He wanted to pull her up on to the bed beside him, but for some reason his limbs weren't quite cooperating.

She grasped his hand and bent her head to touch her forehead to where they joined. He was supposed to be angry with her. He remembered that clearly. But all he could find inside was bliss that she was beside him.

Until she looked up and he realized she was crying. Quietly. Her stoic tears were the most heartbreaking thing he'd ever seen.

"First, I want you to know that I was telling the truth about the document you saw this afternoon. I was writing it all down trying to figure out how to deal with it.

How to help you deal with it. I use words to process things, Gage. That's all it was."

The sincerity in her voice was difficult to argue with. He wanted to believe her, but part of him was reluctant to do that only to find out he'd been had.

"But you were right about the guilt. I did feel guilty. I arranged for us to be together for Cupid week."

She paused, probably waiting for shock. She wouldn't get any. He already knew that.

Just to make sure he completely understood, she clarified, anyway. "I paid to nominate you. I paid to be paired with you."

"I know," he said, the two words slurring out of his mouth uncomfortably. He wanted to say more, but his tongue felt like a useless flap.

"You do? How?"

"Dad let it slip."

"When?" Hope squeezed her eyes shut. "No, never mind. That isn't important. I did it so that I could get the scoop on your story. I had every intention of using our time together to get you to open up."

Gage grunted. It was about all he could manage. His body was rebelling against him. It was taking everything he had to keep his eyelids from slipping shut. What had that nurse given him?

"At first, anyway. And then you came to my house that night after the cocktail party. Upset about something."

"My friend committed suicide." Sure, now his lips wanted to cooperate. He hadn't meant to tell her that.

Her soft green eyes widened with surprise and then crinkled at the corners with sadness. That's one of the things he loved about her. She had such a tough, no-

nonsense exterior, but inside she was nothing but a gooey marshmallow.

He needed a gooey marshmallow to remind him there were still good things in the world. Things worth fighting for.

Her hand brushed across his face. Gage turned into it, prolonging the contact. "I'm so sorry," she whispered.

He shook his head, accepting.

"It didn't take me long to realize I'd made a mistake. I couldn't have used anything you told me to write a story that I knew you didn't want published. I still don't understand why, but that doesn't matter. You've earned your privacy, Gage. You paid for it with every scar on your body.

"But it wasn't just a matter of changing my mind. If that was the case then we could have had a nice time together, reminisced about the good times, finished out the week and both walked away with you never the wiser to my initial ulterior motives."

She glanced away, staring out the open door into the silent corridor. The muscles in her neck strained as she fought against something she didn't want him to see. With unsteady fingers, Gage managed to cup her chin and make her look at him.

Big, fat tears glittered like diamonds in the corners of her eyes. She tried to will them back, but that was a fight not even she could win.

"I spent years telling myself I couldn't love you. I couldn't be just one more girl you took out on Friday night. Your friendship meant too much to me. You meant too much. But you were wild and dangerous, Gage. If there was a rule you wouldn't rest until you'd broken it. You had this…drive. I knew, even back then, that you could hurt me. That letting you in would be just as dangerous as anything you'd ever thought of doing. And twice as stupid."

Gage brushed the pad of his thumb beneath her eye, swiping away the tear that clung there. He didn't want to see her cry.

"I thought you were dead tonight." A sound wheezed out from between her parted lips. "Only for a few minutes, but it was enough. I can't do that. I can't go through that again."

She grasped his hand and pulled it away from her face. Squeezing it, she placed it onto the bed beside him and stood. Her face contorted with pain, she looked down at him.

"I can't stand by and watch you self-destruct, Gage. It hurts too much. Whatever's driving you…I hope you talk to someone about it, because eventually it's going to kill you."

She paused at the door, glancing over her shoulder to look at him one last time.

He wanted to jump out of the bed and stop her. To haul her back against him and explain that the restlessness that drove him disappeared when she was close.

But his body wouldn't listen. The room started graying around the edges. Right before his eyes slammed shut he watched her walk away.

THE MOMENT HE RESURFACED, he rolled over to pull at the tube lodged into his vein. It tied him here and he needed to go after Hope. It was damn difficult considering his right arm had been immobilized against his chest and every movement sent pain lancing through his shoulder. Somehow he managed to fumble the tape off and pull the thing out.

He was one-arming a pair of gray sweats, grumbling beneath his breath the whole time, when his dad walked in the room.

Gage looked up from the string on the sweatpants he was trying to tie with one hand. His dad, big burly man that he was, filled the doorway.

Arms crossed over his chest, the man glared at him. Gage remembered that expression, had seen it more than he liked as a teenager. Had expected it to greet him when he'd arrived home, an undeserving war hero.

"Getting captured and tortured wasn't enough for you? You had to attempt to wrap my Harley around a tree?"

Oh, yeah, his dad was pissed. Although, Gage supposed he really couldn't blame the man. That Harley had been his baby for almost twenty years and he'd totaled the sucker.

With a scowl, his dad crossed the room, swept his hands out of the way and tied his pants for him.

"I think I just lost a million man points." Gage grimaced exaggeratedly, hoping he might be able to joke his way out of this one. "Please don't ever do that again. I'll have the Harley fixed, or replaced, i promise."

"Do you really think I care about the damn bike?"

Gage sank onto the side of the bed, bone-deep exhausted. Not just physically, but mentally and emotionally. He'd been through a lot in the past couple of months and it was finally catching up with him.

"Yes, I think you care about the bike and I think you have every right to care about it. I know how much time and money you put into it."

"Hope was right, you really are an idiot."

Gage's gaze shot to his father's. "You've seen Hope?"

His dad nodded. "She was here to do a piece on the Wilson girl, she has leukemia and needs a bone marrow transplant. They're trying to find a donor."

"Right." Gage's heart sank.

His dad propped against the bed beside him. They were a pair, two grown men, gingerly perched on the edge of a hospital bed, their arms crossed over their chests, staring at the pale green wall rather than look at each other.

"I love you, son."

"I know that, Dad."

"No, apparently you don't. There is nothing in this world, including that damn motorcycle, which I never want to see again, that matters more than you and your sister."

Gage cut his eyes over to his dad. The man was watching him, his face tight and drawn with pointed sincerity. Well.

"When they came to tell us you'd been captured... it was what I'd always expected. Although I imagined it'd be Sheriff Grant making the visit. You were such a difficult boy, always testing boundaries and then leaping flat over them just to prove that you could. I have to admit I was surprised when you made it to eighteen and I thought the army might drive some of that wild outta you."

"Boy, were you wrong."

His dad grunted with wry humor. "Tell me about it. They just paid you to walk that razor's edge. The thing is, you're damn good at doing it, son, and I know

16

HOPE WENT THROUGH the motions. It was Saturday morning and there were several weddings planned for today. The weekends bracketing Valentine's Day were their busiest days. Luckily, the unpredictable South Carolina weather had cooperated and the skies were clear. It also helped that spring was finally starting to poke its head out and the temperature was already in the low 60s. Really pleasant.

She was glad. The brides who'd been waiting for this day deserved everything to be perfect.

The fact that she was having trouble getting into the spirit of things was her problem, not theirs. Luckily, all she had to do was cover the events for the newspaper.

After leaving the hospital, she'd sat her dad down and they'd had a heart-to-heart. She'd told him how unhappy she was running the paper and that she really wanted to spend more time writing.

Her dad admitted that he'd stopped showing up at the office and started letting her handle more at the that. Doesn't make sitting by and watching any easier to take, though."

"That's just about what Hope said."

"Always thought she was a smart girl. Good to her daddy, too. That's one you should marry."

"You been talking to Mama?"

"No. Hope. She loves you and is struggling with the same thing your mama and I have been dealing with since you blew past walking and started runnin' everywhere."

They both chuckled.

"I'm proud of you, son."

The words he'd been waiting his entire life to hear sobered him. Suddenly they weren't enough. Probably because he knew he didn't deserve them.

"You have no idea what I've done," Gage said gutturally.

"I don't need to. I know you. You're a good man."

"I've made mistakes."

"We all do. It's what we do afterward that matters."

They sat there in a charged silence. Gage let his father's words sink in, so similar to what Hope had told him just two nights ago. He wanted to follow their advice, but it was so difficult.

Everyone—including his superior officers and Tanner—had cleared him. He was the only one holding on to the mistake.

Apparently forgiving himself was the hardest part of letting go.

paper in the hope that she wouldn't be able to go. He was afraid she'd leave.

They'd agreed that he'd take back more responsibility, which freed her up for other things. And she'd thrown herself right into her new duties, writing a piece on a local leukemia patient searching for a bone marrow donor. Covering weddings wasn't exactly what she'd anticipated, but they'd needed someone to do it so she'd volunteered.

If she wasn't willing to take any assignment then she didn't deserve the job.

Jenna and Lexi were catering three events today. Willow had designed two of the gowns and the shop she shared with Macey had supplied dresses and tuxes for all of the bridal parties. Tatum was doing all of the flowers at the ceremony and receptions, which meant changing arrangements three times at the gazebo alone.

All of her friends were busy, which she was happy about because all of them could use the business. But it also meant that no one had time to deal with the breakdown she desperately needed.

Walking out of Gage's hospital room yesterday had been the most difficult thing she'd ever done.

Even now, she wasn't entirely certain it had been the right thing to do. But she knew she couldn't survive another visit like Lexi's, thinking he was dead. Like her mother.

It had been too much.

Although, this felt pretty damn terrifying, too.

"Hope," Willow said, walking up beside her and nudging her softly. Until that moment, she hadn't realized the bride and groom were about to start the vows.

The ceremony was half-over. How had she missed it? And what was she supposed to write about?

"Everything all right?" Willow whispered.

Hope nodded. This wasn't the time or place to unload her problems.

Willow gave her a hard look, but shrugged her shoulders and walked away, apparently coming to the same conclusion.

For the next thirty minutes Hope managed to concentrate on the rest of the wedding. The couple was from Hilton Head, so it would be okay if the story was on the short side.

The bride and groom had just walked down the aisle as husband and wife when a commotion broke out at the back of the crowd.

One of the benefits of living in Sweetheart was the opportunity to see all the weddings performed. The raised platform of the gazebo offered everyone a great view of the couple. When the town had decided to build on the image of Sweetheart, a white wood overhang with hand-carved gingerbread had been erected to cover the large area used for an aisle and guests.

Citizens were welcome to attend all weddings performed at the park. That was part of the agreement between the town and the bride and groom. However, everyone was careful to stay on the outskirts of the event, behind the half wall built around the guest area.

Her official capacity as representative from the newspaper allowed her access inside the wall so she wasn't back with everyone else. While weddings at other times of the year weren't always this well-attended, part of the Valentine's festivities included the weddings.

Unfortunately the uproar came from the other side of that wall. Everyone, including the bride and groom, stopped to stare.

Mayor Harper was not going to be happy.

When Gage pushed through a knot of people trying to bar him from entering the guest area, Hope revised her previous statement. Mayor Harper was going to be pissed. Gage knew better.

Despite the frown that twisted her lips, Hope couldn't stop her heart from jerking painfully against her chest. She wondered when the unwelcome reaction would go away.

Gage pushed at someone's hand. Hope was startled when she noticed that his dad was behind him, stopping one of the town council members from reaching for Gage again.

What was going on?

A feeling of dread settled over Hope when Gage vaulted over the wall onto the aisle runner and grimaced in pain. Stupid man. His eyes scanned the crowd. Hope knew before his gaze settled on her that he was looking for her. She wanted to blend into the intricate column behind her, but it was too late to use it as camouflage.

The laser edge of his gaze locked on to her and he moved purposefully through the crowd. At least he paused for a second to speak softly to the bride and groom. They murmured something back to him, but she couldn't hear. Whatever it was, they both turned to look at her. Every head in the place followed them, until she was the focus of hundreds of eyes.

Her face flared with heat, but before she could do anything about it Gage was standing in front of her.

He took the pad of paper she'd been using to make notes and handed it to a woman sitting in the front row. Grasping both of her hands, he pulled her close.

He bent his knees so he could look her straight in the eye and without any preamble said, "I love you." Several people in the front rows clapped, but the response quickly died when she didn't say anything.

Hope could feel the heat of him, warm and tempting. It would be so easy to give in to what she wanted, to just accept what he was offering her. But the words weren't enough and she wasn't sure they ever would be.

"Did you hear me?" he asked. "I love you."

"I heard you," she said from between numb lips.

"I love you, Hope Rawlings. Will you marry me?"

Oh, God. Every girl dreams about hearing those words. Hope certainly had, although the guy asking them had always been fuzzy. In none of the scenarios that she'd played with had she ever felt it necessary to say no. But she did.

The same people that had clapped now gasped.

"What do you mean 'no'?"

Frustrated with him and with herself, Hope pulled her hands away from him and threw them up into the air. "You've been home for less than two weeks, Gage."

"Okay," he said in an agreeable voice that grated against her already-frayed nerves. "I don't care what circumstances brought us together. I want the chance to prove to us both that this is real. Will you let me do that?"

Hope could practically feel every person crowded into the space take a collective breath and hold it. They were waiting. Gage was waiting. Her chest hurt, so tight with the tension fighting a battle inside her. She wanted to say yes, but she just couldn't.

The same fear and sense of self-preservation she'd used against him all those years ago made her say, "No."

Gage's wounded eyes nearly killed her. She almost took the word back…but she couldn't.

"Why are you doing this? I know you love me. Why is it so hard for you to take a chance? To say yes?"

Pain, fear and unhappiness mixed inside her. They made her want to tear her own skin off. She didn't like living inside this person, but she couldn't… "I hate myself for saying no, Gage, but I have to. I can't live waiting for the next phone call or visit to tell me that you're dead. I want to be strong enough to handle that. But I'm not. There are only two ways this ends."

She held up two fingers and ticked them off. "You dead and me absolutely destroyed. Or both of us miserable because I can't live with who you are. Neither of those scenarios is worth the agony and risk."

A GLIMMER OF HOPE LIT the center of his chest. Maybe, just maybe, he could diffuse this situation and fix everything.

Reaching for her, he pulled Hope into the shelter of his arms and whispered into her ear, "I called you a coward once."

She stiffened.

"I take it back. You're stronger than you give yourself credit for, Hope. I know you think you're making the right decision—the tough decision—but you aren't."

She struggled in his arms, but he refused to relinquish his hold. After years of wanting and fighting for her, he wasn't letting Hope get away that easily. She was scared. He got that. He'd been there, uncertain that he could take one more cut, needle prick or blow to the face. But he'd found the strength, somewhere. And he'd do it again, find that reserve that lurked deep inside and give it all to her. Because he loved her. Because she needed it.

"And I'll tell you why. That thing that drives me, that craves the risk and the danger and the reward, it disappears when I'm with you, Hope. You…quiet everything inside of me. When you're near I don't need anything but you."

Hope buried her head against his good shoulder and made a muffled sound. He tried to pull her away so he could see her face, but with only one arm he couldn't do it. So he let her rest there, against him. Slowly, the warmth of her seeped inside of him and the panic he'd been fighting since she walked out of his hospital room dimmed.

"What about the army, Gage? I want to tell you I can deal with it, but I can't. I just…can't." Her words were hidden against him, as if she didn't want to face them or the fear they represented.

"I've already decided not to re-up and that had nothing to do with you. It's time. I won't let men put their lives in my hands if I can't promise them everything I have to protect them. And after what happened…I'm too unpredictable out there. I might be willing to risk my own life, but I won't risk anyone else's."

Her arms tightened around him, slowly she pulled away to stare up at him, a mix of hope and fear clouding her eyes.

Gage ran his thumb down her cheek. "Risking everything was easy before you. Now I have too much to lose—you, a life together, a chance at something solid and happy."

Gage willed her to hear him, to really listen to what he was telling her.

"I have something strong and real with you, Hope. The only thing that scares me is losing it. Losing you. Please don't throw away what we have. Not now. Not after everything we've been through to get here."

Hope swallowed. Her eyes welled with tears and Gage thought he'd really lost.

Until in a tremulous voice she said, "Yes."

Someone at the back of the crowd whooped.

Gage said, "Would you say that again?"

Hope grinned, the corners of her eyes wrinkling even as the tears fell. "Yes," she yelled, throwing back her head and raising her voice so that everyone could hear her.

"Yes, what?" he asked.

"Yes, I want a life with you. Yes, I love you."

"Yes, you'll marry me?"

She paused for several seconds, searching his face. "Yes, I'll marry you."

With one arm, Gage pulled her close. Everyone around them erupted with laughter and applause. The sound nearly drowned out his last question, but the only person who mattered heard it.

"Yes, you'll never tell me no again?"

"Don't push it," Hope whispered back, a wicked gleam filling her eyes.

She wrapped her arms around his neck and kissed

him hard. Agony burned through his shoulder and Gage couldn't bite back a gasp of pain. Hope's eyes widened with horror. He collapsed onto the nearest chair, dropping his head and cradling his wounded shoulder until the throb subsided.

"Gage!" she groaned, remorse thickening her voice. Bending down to him, she hovered. "What can I do?"

He looked up at her, freshly overwhelmed by the realization that she was his. Finally.

"Come here."

Hope shrieked with surprise when he reached for her and tumbled her into his lap. Her body sprawled across him. She immediately started to squirm, no doubt afraid that she was hurting him more. Even if she had been, the ache would have been worth it.

He joined their mouths again, diving into her and taking exactly what he wanted. Her body melted against him. Her hands searched, finding purchase in the hair at the nape of his neck. She tugged, finding a better angle to bring them together. Although this time she was careful not to touch his bad shoulder.

Around them people coughed, whistled and mumbled crude suggestions.

After several seconds, Hope pulled away, breathless. She trembled, the fine quiver something only he could feel. Her skin was pink, with desire and embarrassment, as she buried her face into the crook of his good shoulder.

"Everyone's watching."

He didn't care. Now that he'd turned over a new leaf the town was just going to have to get used to seeing him with his hands all over Hope. Better that than letting goats run inside the high school.

Besides, they were a good advertisement. Sweetheart, South Carolina, where Cupid always wins.

No question, he was the victor this time. "Let them," he growled, finding her mouth and asking for more.

* * * * *